Also by Peter Lefcourt

The Woody
Abbreviating Ernie
Di and I
The Dreyfus Affair
The Deal

Peter Lefcourt

Eleven Karens

A Novel

Simon & Schuster
New York · London · Toronto · Sydney · Singapore

SIMON & SCHUSTER
Rockefeller Center
1230 Avenue of the Americas
New York, NY 10020

This book is a work of fiction. Names, characters,
places, and incidents either are products of the
author's imagination or are used fictitiously. Any
resemblance to actual events or locales or persons,
living or dead, is entirely coincidental.

Designed by Lauren Simonetti

For information regarding special discounts for bulk purchases, please contact Simon &
Schuster Special Sales at 1-800-456-6798 or business@simonandschuster.com

Manufactured in the United States of America
10 9 8 7 6 5 4 3 2 1

Library of Congress Cataloging-in-Publication Data
Lefcourt, Peter.
    Eleven Karens: a novel/Peter Lefcourt.
    p.   cm.
    1. Man-woman relationships—Fiction. I. Title.
PS3562.E3737   E44   2003
813'.54—dc21   2002021792
ISBN 0-684-87034-7

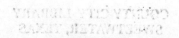

For Terri, the ultimate Karen

I lie in order to tell the truth.

—duc de La Rochefoucauld

Eleven Karens

WHY

M*ost men remember* the women in their lives with some sort of confused mixture of tenderness, nostalgia, and regret. I remember the women in mine as Karens. While no two other women with whom I have been involved share the same name—no multiple Janes, Marys, or Roxannes—eleven of them were named Karen.

I spoke to several of the mental health professionals I have consulted over the years (two of whom were named Ivan) about this predilection for Karens. They provided me with various theories about how my particular neuroses contributed to this chronic Karenphilia. I won't bore you with details here except to say that they all mentioned some element of self-destructiveness on my part.

I asked a friend who makes his living as a statistician what the odds were against being involved with eleven women all named Karen in one lifetime. The first thing he wanted to know, naturally, was the size of the statistical sample. I told him the number. Though it's a perfectly respectable number, I have no idea where it falls on the scale for men of my age, height, weight, and social background. It is a modest (though not insignificant) number—a number, let's just say, that would fall somewhere in between Wilt Chamberlain's[1] number and St. Paul's[2] number.

---

[1]The late NBA star and sexual athlete, who claimed to have had sex with over 10,000 women in his lifetime.
[2]Greek erotophobe and apostle, whose idea of a good time was a donkey ride to Damascus.

He told me the odds were on the order of 29,976 to 1 against. In order to have a basis for comparison, I asked him for some similarly improbable phenomena. He cited the following examples: being hit by two navy blue Volvo convertibles within fifteen months' time in two separate cities; getting food poisoning from seven consecutive fast-food hamburgers in seven different fast-food restaurants on seven different days; being hit by a foul ball off the bat of a left-handed pinch hitter in the sixth inning of three different baseball games in three different stadiums within a five-month period; and, my least favorite, getting four STD's from four different women in four separate states west of the Mississippi within any given four-year period.

As you can see, we're dealing with a long shot here. There's obviously something going on that cannot be explained by either abnormal psychology or probability theory. Which leaves religion.

So I tried e-mailing a Reform rabbi and ex-fraternity brother about this. He replied by telling me about an Old Testament prophet named Ephrhahim, who had nine children who all drowned in wells. When I questioned the applicability of this story to my situation, he told me that God works in mysterious ways and that I needed to "just go with it."

Einstein, who was a lapsed Jew, maintained that God doesn't play dice with the universe. I think he was dead wrong. I think He plays fast and loose with us. How else do you explain James Dean blindsiding Donald Turnipseed on an empty highway on a sunny day in California, Bill Buckner letting a feeble ground ball go through his legs in the '86 World Series, the Immaculate Conception, Calvin Coolidge, or having eleven Karens in your life?

I suppose you could ask the Karens themselves what attracted them to me and see if you could establish some coherence from that perspective. But, first, you would have to track them down. They are on three different continents, scattered to the winds, and one, at least, is on a planet of her very own.

And so over the years I have grown to accept this skewing of the numbers as just another manifestation of the arbitrary nature of the universe. If you flip a coin a hundred times and get heads, the chances are still fifty-fifty that you'll flip heads the hundred and first time. Every time I meet a new woman, the odds are the same that she'll be a Karen. I just go with it.

What follows, then, is the narrative of my odyssey among the Karens. Some were brief affairs, others were longer relationships. One was a one-night stand. But they are all there embedded in the hard drive of memory and in the space in our hearts that we reserve for the women we've loved in our lives.

The best way to remember something is to write about it. So I decided to write a book. And this is the book I wrote.

I
THE HAIR JOB

There was always a Karen, even before the first one. There was a past-life Karen and a prenatal Karen, and a Karen who took me from my mother to lay me down gently in the bassinet in the hospital where I was born.

And there were undoubtedly Karens who took care of me from time to time in my very early years, who spelled my mother when she was tired, who played with me, bathed me with tenderness, took me for walks, holding on to one hand as I tottered along exploring my universe.

But the first Karen in my life was none of these. She has the distinction of being not only the first one I slept with but the first one I married. When I tell you that this Karen was named Karen Shrummer and that I knew her in the fifth grade, you'll accuse me of lying.

Of course I'm lying. Reread the epigraph.

I can see her now, sitting at the desk near the wardrobe, her hands folded in front of her, waiting for Mrs. Murtaugh to dismiss us. Mrs. Murtaugh was red-haired, pallid, a woman whose patience had been honed thin by too many years of teaching the fifth grade in a New York City public school. She slapped me once, good and hard, when I was horsing around with Kenny Birnbaum, my best man, in the back of the class.

Tell you the truth, I don't blame her for whacking me. I can only imagine what a dull headache at 3:20 in the afternoon of a hot early-June day in a school in Queens in the mid-fifties felt like. You're ten minutes from peace and quiet, from a mentholated Salem in the teachers' lounge, and two boys are loudly playing knights on horseback in the back of the classroom.

I took the blow well, managing to stay mounted on Kenny Birnbaum's shoulders. When Mrs. Murtaugh, losing it entirely, started to screech, I calmly dismounted and returned to my desk, running the gauntlet of girls with their hands folded in front of them, hearing a collective intake of breath, a palpable fluttering coming from them.

This incident earned me a bad-boy reputation in the class, a reputation that I did not entirely deserve but one that I was in no rush to disclaim. From that moment on it was clear to the fifth grade girls that I was a threat to civilized society. I would have to be domesticated. I'm convinced that that was the moment in which they decided to marry me off to Karen Shrummer.

Why Karen Shrummer? Why not Denise Demarco? Or Bonnie Baer? Or, for that matter, why not that fetching little strumpet Bertha Haas, who went to parties in costume jewelry and with a dab of her mother's Shalimar behind her ears?

I had dark thoughts about Bertha Haas, but I don't think I would have married her. You didn't marry Bertha Haas. Karen Shrummer, on the other hand, was the girl you took the long walk down the aisle with.

Still, I wasn't envisaging getting married to anyone yet. I had plans. I wanted to be a shortstop for the Dodgers, then maybe go out west and herd cattle in Montana. At that point in my life I didn't see settling down to TV and pot roast with Karen Shrummer or with any other girl.

But it made little difference what I wanted. Once the decision had been made to marry me off to Karen Shrummer, I was a marked man.

The parties we had in the fifth grade were organized by the girls. We showed up, hair slicked back, starched white assembly shirts, in sweat socks and shiny shoes, and hovered around the Cracker Jacks and Pepsi while the girls congregated in the other corner, admiring one another's dresses and occasionally walking over and dragging one of us off to dance.

All of this, of course, was just prelude. Around ten o'clock we got down to business. Business consisted of prepubescent kissing games that were played out in a darkened corner of someone's knotty-pine finished basement to the strains of Johnny Mathis[3] from the portable RCA Victrola.

The two principal games were Spin the Bottle and Post Office. Spin the Bottle was the less interesting of the two. It was played out in public: You had to kiss the girl in front of everybody else, which provided for the girls a sense of collective triumph and for us a sort of collective humiliation. But Post Office was strictly down and dirty. With Post Office you got to do it alone in a closet in the dark.

The way it worked was that somebody would say they had a letter for you from a girl, and then you marched off into the closet with that girl, often taller than you, and either kissed her or stood there counting to sixty. You would have thought that they could have come up with a more imaginative way of getting a boy and a girl alone in a dark space.

I had gotten letters before from Karen Shrummer and had a vague memory of soft lips with a cool aftertaste of peppermint Life Savers.

---

[3]Popular singer of the era, best known for his "make out music," notably "Wonderful, Wonderful," "Chances Are," and "The Twelfth of Never."

But her letters weren't like the letters you got from Bertha Haas. Those letters left you dizzy. After you got a letter from Bertha Haas you needed a moment to compose yourself before wobbling out of the closet to face the disapproval of the girls.

*   *   *

On the Saturday night in June after I got slugged by Mrs. Murtaugh, there was a party at Denise Demarco's. I wound up getting more letters from Karen Shrummer than I had ever gotten before. We marched off together to the closet and locked lips for sixty seconds at a time. A minute is a long time to stand there with your lips pressed against someone without doing something with your hands, but your hands would get slapped down if they wandered. And forget doing anything with your tongue. If you got cute with your tongue, they'd bite it off.

Nevertheless, that night, after getting the third letter from her, I found my hands wandering a little up her back, if only to break the monotony of what was degenerating into a simple act of physical stamina. She didn't stop me. Instead she put her hands on the back of my neck and did the hair thing.

Remember the hair thing? Movie actresses would run their hands through the back of a man's hair. Your mother would be watching *Million Dollar Movie* on television and break into a hot sweat when Loretta Young would run her hands through Jeff Chandler's hair.

I walked out of that closet a little wobbly, not unlike like the way I walked out after getting a letter from Bertha Haas. This wobbliness, however, was clearly acceptable to the other girls. They had baited the trap, and I had bit hard.

From that point on, I was a dead man.

In the cafeteria at lunchtime there seemed to be an inordinate amount of attention directed at me. I'd be about to blow my straw into Larry Burkhardt's face when I'd notice the girls watching me from the next table. I'd look over and see them, with their neatly wrapped Velveeta-cheese sandwiches, surrounding their candidate, Karen Shrummer, who sat there with a self-satisfied look on her face.

Then there was the school bus. I found that there was usually only one seat available, the one beside Karen Shrummer. So we rode home together, silently, eyes straight ahead. In retrospect I can see the inexorability of the series of events that unfolded that June which would lead me to the altar. But at the time I was clueless.

One day I had the following conversation with Kenny Birnbaum. We were in his basement playing Ping-Pong when he suddenly asked, "You like Karen Shrummer?"

"Uh-uh," I protested.

"So how come you're getting married to her?"

"What are you talking about?"

"After school ends. In Bonnie Baer's garage."

"Get out of here."

"It's not true?"

"Kenny, don't you think I'd know about it if I was getting married? I mean, I'd have to get a suit."

"But if you were getting married, I'd be your best man, right?"

"Yeah. Sure."

"I was the best man at my brother Nathan's wedding last summer. I got to hold the ring."

"There's not going to be any wedding, okay?"

I served, low and hard, with a lot of topspin.

"Three serving zero . . ."

*   *   *

That week was the annual class trip to the Museum of Natural History in Manhattan. There was an hour bus ride from Queens, and I found myself, big surprise, beside Karen Shrummer.

We rode in silence till we got to Queens Boulevard and she offered me a Life Saver. I took it, noncommittally, like Rory Calhoun[4] accepting a cup of coffee from the schoolmarm, and went back to staring at the back of the seat in front of us.

She broke the silence just before we went through the Midtown Tunnel. "I'm going to Howe Caverns with my family on Saturday."

"Oh."

"What are you doing on Saturday?"

"Nothing."

"You ever been to Howe Caverns?"

"No."

We entered the dark, vaginal interior of the Queens-Midtown Tunnel, and I looked out the window at the cops sealed in the glass booths and thought they had great jobs. Which will give you some idea of where my mind was at the moment.

We were still in the tunnel when she said, "My sister can't go because she has hives, so my mother said I could bring a friend."

"Oh."

"So do you want to go?"

She had me. I had already admitted to never having been there and to having no plans for Saturday. So I nodded, said something vague, which I thought had been, at best, noncommittal. But by the time we got to the museum the assignation had been communicated to the other girls. There was more than the usual amount of

---

[4]Movie actor (1922–1999), star of eighty-two films, among them *A Ticket to Tomahawk*, *Motel Hell*, and *Won Ton Ton, the Dog who Saved Hollywood*.

whispering among the Sisterhood as we trudged past the big birch-bark canoe and the other American Indian exhibits.

In the cafeteria, Kenny Birnbaum sat down next to me and said, "So you're going to Howe Caverns with Karen Shrummer Saturday?"

"Who told you?"

"Everybody knows."

"Her sister has hives."

* * *

The Shrummers picked me up in their new 1956 Chevy Impala at 8 o'clock Saturday morning. Gordon and Marilyn Shrummer sat in the front in Bermuda shorts, smoking Old Golds with the windows open, and Karen Shrummer sat in the back, burrowed into a corner, wearing dungarees with the cuffs rolled up, a sweatshirt, and sneakers.

We took the Triborough Bridge into Manhattan, then the West Side Highway to the Sawmill River Parkway to the Taconic State Parkway north.

Gordon Shrummer drove with maddening regularity, keeping the speedometer needle right on 50, one hand on the Impala's enamel steering wheel, the other hand holding the Old Gold. Karen Shrummer and I weren't talking until Marilyn said, "Awfully quiet back there."

So we talked about school, running out of gas after a couple of minutes and going the rest of the way in unpunctuated silence.

It was 11:30 when we got to Howe Caverns. The sun had burned off the cloud layer, and it was hot. Still, we were told to bring sweaters with us down into the cavern, where the temperature supposedly went as low as 58 degrees Fahrenheit.

We followed Gordon and Marilyn down the stone stairs into the belly of the cavern. For a while it was single file, and I was behind Karen Shrummer walking down the steps.

At ten and a half Karen Shrummer did not yet have a woman's body. As I recall. There may have been tiny breastlets under the sweatshirt, maybe even a training bra, but that would have been the extent of it. But I have to tell you I can still remember what she looked like from the back in dungarees walking down narrow stone steps into cold weather. That image goes into the Oldies but Goodies Hall of Fame, alongside such early entries as Maria Schell dancing for Yul Brynner in *The Brothers Karamazov* and Brigitte Bardot sunbathing nude in *And God Created Woman*.

But the day itself, as far as I was concerned, was a lead balloon. When you've seen one stalactite, you've seen them all. There was an endless geology lecture and a trip through the souvenir shop, where Gordon bought a collection of color slides, which he no doubt showed to captive audiences in his finished basement. We had hamburgers and french fries in a little cafeteria down below, shivering in our sweaters, and then took the long climb back up.

On the way back to the car, Gordon put his arm around my shoulders and said, "Wasn't that great?"

"Yeah," I said.

"Nature made that thousands of years ago."

"Uh-huh."

"It'll be around for your children and their children too, won't it?"

"Sure . . ."

When we got in the car, Marilyn said, "Now stop chattering away so much back there, you two." Gordon laughed. Karen Shrummer and I didn't.

It was a long drive home. Between the heat, the hamburgers, and the monotonous drone of the Impala's engine locked into its 50 mph cadence, I fell asleep before we reached the city. I reawoke as Gordon handed the guy in the Triborough Bridge tollbooth a quarter, and when I did I discovered Karen Shrummer's head resting on my shoulder. She jerked awake, as if she too had been asleep for a while.

Did her head drift unconsciously onto my shoulder in her sleep? I would never know. We quickly separated, each of us flushed and not risking a look at the other one. But the fact remained that we had fallen asleep together in the back of the car.

Then we heard Gordon say loudly to Marilyn, clearly for our benefit, "Well, Marilyn, it looks like those two are just going to have to get married, since they've already slept together."

"You bet," Marilyn replied, and the two of them had a long, loud laugh at our expense.

I couldn't even look at Karen Shrummer till her father pulled the Impala up in front of our house and I turned and mumbled a hasty "see you." Then I uttered my thank-yous to Gordon and Marilyn and got out of the car. The Impala, already sporting its WE'VE BEEN TO HOWE CAVERNS sticker, backed out of the driveway.

*   *   *

The first thing that Kenny Birnbaum said to me on the way to school Monday morning was, "You really sleep with Karen Shrummer?"

There was only one possible source for the story, and she wasn't meeting my eyes. Not even in the cafeteria, where I made it a point to stare right at her, as if to say, "Excuse me, it was bad enough having to listen to that cretin of a father of yours in his Bermuda shorts make bad jokes, but must the entire fifth grade of P.S. 26 be in on this as well?"

I was helpless in the wake of the story. She had obviously told everyone about her father's little joke, and it was the joke that created the momentum for the inevitable next step. The marriage. I'm convinced that without the joke the marriage might not have been possible.

The first I heard of the marriage was, once again, from Kenny Birnbaum, whom the girls were obviously using as a conduit to me. I assumed he thought he was being funny when he said to me, "I guess you got to marry her now, huh?"

We were opening bubble gum packages to see what baseball cards we had when he made this bizarre statement.

"What're you talking about?"

"Karen Shrummer. You can't sleep with her and not marry her, can you?"

"Would you come off it, Kenny," I said, and started shuffling through the cards. "You want Bobby Shantz?"[5]

"Got him. Her father's going to come after you with a shotgun."

"All I did was fall asleep in the car on the way back from Howe Caverns, okay? You got Allie Reynolds?"[6]

"Uh-uh. I'll give you Snider[7] for him."

"You'll give me the Duke for Allie Reynolds?"

"I got two of them. . . . If you did it I could be the best man."

---

[5]Pitcher, Philadelphia Athletics, 1949–1954; bats right, throws left; born Pottstown, Pennsylvania, September 26, 1925; 537 games; 1,938 innings pitched; W 119, L 99; 3.38 ERA.

[6]Pitcher, New York Yankees, 1942–1954, bats right, throws right; born Bethany, Oklahoma, February 10, 1915; 2,492 innings pitched; W 182, L 107; 3.30 ERA.

[7]Edwin Donald Snider, Brooklyn Dodgers, 1947–57, Los Angeles Dodgers, 1958–62, bats left, throws right; born Los Angeles, California, September 19, 1926; 2,143 games; 7,161 AB; 2,116 hits; 407 HR.

"Kenny, I'm ten and a half. You don't get married at ten and a half."

"They do so. In Kentucky."

"You got to be at least sixteen, even in Kentucky."

"Uh-uh. Herbie Karp said he heard that an eight-year-old girl had a baby in Kentucky."

I didn't even know why I was having this conversation with Kenny Birnbaum. He was a notorious disseminator of misinformation. He had told me that after his heart attack President Eisenhower had a secret battery-powered artificial heart put in that only Mamie and the CIA knew about and that they had to plug him into the wall every night while he slept to recharge the battery.

"Look, I'm not getting married, okay?"

But even as I stood there trading baseball cards with Kenny Birnbaum plans were being made. The Sisterhood was hard at work. The date was being set. The venue chosen. The bride's wardrobe discussed.

As June progressed and the weather got hotter, we sat in class with the windows wide open and gazed longingly out at the parched grass, waiting for school to be over.

One day, a few minutes from dismissal, there was an air-raid drill. We had to file out into the hallway and sit there in silence, our heads down in our laps, our arms over them protectively. As if our arms could save us from the radiation the Russians were dropping on us.

I found myself next to Louise Leventhal, a skinny girl with stringy black hair and an overbite. When Mrs. Murtaugh was down at the other end of the hall, looking impatiently at the clock, waiting for her deliverance, Louise Leventhal turned to me and whispered, "Saturday afternoon. Three o'clock. Bonnie Baer's garage."

"What?" I whispered back.

"The wedding," she whispered, louder. Mrs. Murtaugh's head turned toward us. Louise Leventhal put her head back under her arms.

On the school bus home, Karen Shrummer was sitting with Louise Leventhal. I got stuck next to Bonnie Baer because Kenny Birnbaum's mother had picked him at school up for his monthly allergy shot.

"What are you going to wear?" she asked me.

"What do you mean, wear?"

"You should wear at least a sport jacket. And don't wear sneakers, okay?"

"I don't know if I can come."

"You better be there," she said.

All that week, these types of peremptory conversations took place. Various girls would approach me with wardrobe suggestions, questions about the ring, admonitions about showing up and being on time.

Kenny Birnbaum had by now openly defected. He started obsessing about the ring. I had to have a ring, he kept saying. Time was running out.

He dragged me down to Union Turnpike after school to scour the Cafoutas' Five-and-Dime store for something appropriate. They had costume jewelry there, but the cheapest ring was a buck seventy-five, and I wasn't blowing seven weeks' worth of allowances to give to a girl in some shotgun ceremony in Bonnie Baer's garage.

He said, fine, he'd buy the ring. He was the one who was supposed to hold it anyway, and it made no difference who actually bought it, did it? All I had to do was put it on her finger.

"What if I won't do it?" I asked.

"You have to. You have to have a ring when you get married."

"What if I won't get married?"

He looked at me, his eyes watery from sneezing, and said, "You got to."

"Why?"

"Because . . ."

It was clear to him that I had to because *somebody* had to. And I was the one they had chosen to do this. So it had to be done.

News of my recalcitrance was evidently reported to the Sisterhood because they decided to roll out the heavy artillery. That afternoon they made sure to have Karen Shrummer next to me on the bus.

She was wearing a yellow seersucker dress and open-toed black shoes, her hair tied up with a red ribbon. Even at three o'clock in the afternoon, you could still smell the Ivory soap on her.

As usual, we didn't say much. But as she was getting off, the stop before mine, her hand reached over, ostensibly to hold on to the back of the seat for balance, and as it did, her hand brushed the back of my head.

"Sorry," she said, regaining her balance, and continuing past Bonnie Baer, Louise Leventhal, and Denise Demarco.

It was a hit-and-run hair job. No doubt about it. She had gotten off that bus every day without balancing herself on the back of the seat.

Anyway, that was Friday, the day before the wedding. That evening I was interrupted at dinner by two phone calls. The first one was from Kenny Birnbaum.

"I'm eating," I said, into the hall phone.

"The condemned man ate a hearty meal."

But the second phone call was the one that counted. It was from Karen Shrummer.

"Hi," she said.

"Hi," I replied.

There was a long pause. Finally she said, "You really want to do this tomorrow, don't you?"

I didn't know what to say. I really had no idea what I wanted at that moment.

What I heard in her voice was fear. Fear that I wouldn't show up, fear that she would be there all alone, stood up at the altar, in front of the entire Sisterhood, whose exemplar she was.

Somewhere in the hard wiring, there was a better part of me. Or a worse. I'm not sure. For all I know, it could have been the hair job, but I said, "Yes."

* * *

I didn't leave my first Karen standing at the altar. Not only did I show up but I showed up wearing my one and only sport jacket, a blue-and-white plaid, and my Thom McAn brown shoes.

Bonnie Baer's garage was decorated with crepe paper for the occasion. The entire Sisterhood was present. Some girl had dragged Larry Burkhardt along. He and Kenny Birnbaum and I were the only boys.

The girls had worked hard to make the garage look like a wedding chapel. There was an aisle created with a dozen bridge chairs, six on each side. They had thrown a couple of old sheets over Bonnie Baer's father's snow tires and lawn mower. There was a portable record player plugged in to the electric socket that Bonnie Baer's father must have plugged his soldering iron into.

Though I would have preferred her in dungarees, Karen Shrummer looked terrific in somebody's sister's white communion dress with somebody's mother's white veil and a pair of white pumps, at least a size too big for her.

It was very well organized, from start to finish. Kenny Birnbaum and I walked down the aisle to a scratchy Mendelssohn. We stood in front of a folding stack table and waited for the "Here Comes the Bride" part of the Wedding March.

Larry Burkhardt had been drafted to give the bride away. What did they have on *him*? I wondered. To his credit, he did it without smirking, but you could tell he had better things to do with his Saturday afternoon than watch one of his own take the pipe.

He walked down the aisle with Karen Shrummer looking as if he was at his grandmother's funeral. I stood gaping at her, swept up in the white vision in front of me, momentarily paralyzed until Bonnie Baer whispered loudly, "You have to go meet her."

I walked toward her; then Karen Shrummer herself turned me around and put her arm on mine. We walked another ten feet and we were in front of the stack table.

Bonnie Baer took out a piece of paper and read the whole ceremony. Dearly beloved. We are gathered here together. Do you? Do you? Does anybody here object? And so forth. By the book. Verbatim from every wedding you've even seen on TV.

I stood there, a deer in the headlights, and gave the appropriate answers. At the crucial moment, Kenny Birnbaum dropped the $1.75 ring, which rolled under the snow tires and had to be retrieved.

When Bonnie Baer told me that I could kiss the bride, I could sense the collective breathlessness of the Sisterhood. This was it, the sanctification, the point to the whole exercise.

I moved in, Casanova with a hair lick, and tasted the peppermint and warm breath of my bride. The back of my head waited for a hair job. In vain.

There would be no hair job then, or at any time in the future, from Karen Shrummer. She didn't need to do hair jobs anymore. I had walked down the aisle; I had put the ring on her finger.

As soon as it was over, as soon as Mendelssohn ground to a halt and the girls all gathered around Karen Shrummer to congratulate her, Kenny Birnbaum, Larry Burkhardt, and I made our escape. We went home, got into sneakers and jeans, and twenty minutes later we were back on the street playing stickball, whistling in the dark, as if nothing had happened.

But we each knew that something profound had happened that afternoon in Bonnie Baer's garage. We didn't know exactly what it was, but it lay there undigested in the pits of our stomachs. We danced through the stickball game like ghostly figures. We were dead men, moving in slow motion.

*   *   *

I went to camp that summer, tried to feel up a few sixth-grade girls, with no success. When I got back to school next year Karen Shrummer barely gave me the time of day. She was going out with some guy in the seventh grade who wore a leather jacket and pegged pants. The parties became less frequent and were relatively sober affairs. We watched movies and played charades. The post office had shut down for good.

There should, of course, be an asterisk next to Karen Shrummer's name. The same clinical standard was not applied to her as it was to the others. You may think I was just padding my numbers by including her. But that would be beside the point.

She remains a Karen, nonetheless. The first Karen. La Prima. She set the standard. She left her fingerprints on my heart.

II
THIRD BASE

If the fifth grade is a caldron, high school is a volcano. Surviving one does not necessarily prepare you for surviving the other. The lava just keeps floating downstream. You learn to swim upstream as fast as you can with your mouth closed.

Between the ages of ten and fifteen, I had no Karens in my life. There was merely a blur of girls passing me by, trailing the lingering scent of forbidden pleasure. I suffered in silence, inching backward, boats against the current, as F. Scott says, in the hope that there would come a day again when somebody would want to take me into a dark closet.

When that day came, I was completely unprepared for it.

My second Karen showed up during my sophomore year at Jamaica High School, in Queens. She was a cheerleader and cute as a button. An inch at most above five feet, with a ponytail down between her shoulders and a small, pert dancer's body.

I first laid eyes on her at a swim meet that I was covering as a cub reporter for the school newspaper, *The Hilltopper.*[8] Covering the swimming team was relegated to the rookie on the staff. You had to spend hours at the pool below the gym, an ugly overheated room that reeked of chlorine and sweat, reporting on events that nobody cared about.

Attendance was sparse. Basketball and football were the star

---

[8]The school was on top of a hill.

sports. Reporting on a swim meet was largely a matter of recounting who won the race and in what time. Moreover, when you were writing about the swimming team it was extremely taxing to come up with the variety of metaphoric adjectives that high school journalism encourages. If the basketball team had a number of names, like the Cagers, or the Five, or the Hoopsters, the swimming team had only one, the Mermen.

"The Jamaica Mermen swam to a crushing victory against the Richmond Hill swimmers today. . . ."

The cheerleaders were required to show up at the swim meets. You could tell that they didn't want to be there. The humidity made their hair frizzy and their makeup run. And there wasn't a lot of room beside the pool for elaborate choreography. They had to stand in front of the bleachers occupied exclusively by the Mermen's mothers and the *Hilltopper* reporter and shout:

> Step on the starter
> Crank up the Lizzie
> Come on Jamaica
> Let's get busy.

I would sit there with my notebook, copy the list of races, and wait for the times to be posted. Naturally, I spent a lot of time watching the cheerleaders and, a fortiori, Karen Szbachevsky.

Being small and light, Karen Szbachevsky was always at the top of the human pyramid. She stepped nimbly on the boy cheerleaders' shoulders, waving her megaphone gracefully in the air, literally on top of the world.

From where I sat, in the fourth and top row of the bleachers, I was more or less on the same eye level as her. And it was at those times that we made visual contact. She was up there for maybe five seconds, so our contact was quick and intense.

Whether Karen Szbachevsky was interested in me or not, however, was hard to determine. All I had to go by were those brief moments, those shutter-clicks of time, when it appeared to me that she was looking straight at me.

So I decided to try an experiment. For the next swim meet, against John Adams High School, I moved down a row and to the right, from where she would have to lower her eyes and swivel them to her left to see me.

Unfortunately, things did not go well for the home team. The Mermen were getting blown out of the water by John Adams, and there wasn't a lot of opportunity for cheering. Still, the cheerleaders had shown up; they were there breathing in the chlorine and the sweat, so eventually they did the pyramid number. Karen Szbachevsky climbed lightly up on the top and, at first, looked toward the spot where I usually sat. Then she lowered her eyes, turned them to her left, and locked right into mine.

My heart skidded to a complete stop. I didn't breathe again until she hopped lightly down, threw up her arms and shouted, "Step on the starter/Crank up the Lizzie . . ."

The rest of the meet was a blur. My editor complained the next day that I had misspelled the names of half the John Adams swimmers. And he didn't like my headline: SECOND PRESIDENT MANHANDLES MERMEN.

The truth was I wrote the whole thing going to school the next day on the bus. Immediately following the meet, instead of verifying the list of swimmers' names with their coach, as I was supposed to, I followed Karen Szbachevsky out of the gym.

She left with two other cheerleaders—the Blumenthal twins,

Bobbi and Sandi—without so much as a glance in my direction. The Blumenthals were identical twins, both blond and fleshy, with full mouths and limpid eyes and virtually impossible to tell apart. The word on them was that they put out.

The three of them, coats over their cheerleading uniforms, headed down the hill. I followed them to the bus stop on Hillside Avenue and waited while they went into a drugstore for twenty minutes. It was November and already dark and cold. I was freezing my ass off in my letterless Jamaica High School windbreaker, no hat, no gloves.

Karen Szbachevsky said good-bye to the Blumenthals and walked across the street to wait for the Q-17. The Q-17 was a bad bus. It was a bus you didn't want to have to take. It went east along Hillside, then turned south to South Jamaica, then east again to St. Albans—tough, working-class neighborhoods that, for me, were terra incognita.

I stood across the street, hidden in a store entrance, until I saw the Q-17 two traffic lights away. I waited for it to pass the first light, then, timing the bus as if it were a freight train I was trying to hop, I ran recklessly across Hillside Avenue and got on just before the door closed.

She was in the back of the bus, her nose buried in *A Tale of Two Cities*. I walked nonchalantly to the rear of the bus, sat down beside her, and announced, "It was the best of times, it was the worst of times."

She looked up at me with a very serious, but not surprised, look and said, "I can't figure out how it can be both the best and the worst of times, can you?"

"Pathetic fallacy," I replied glibly.

"Do you know what happens to Sydney Carton?"

"Yeah."

"You read the whole book *already*?"

"Uh-huh," I lied. I had skipped to the end and read the "'tis a far, far better thing that I do" speech Sydney Carton does in front of the guillotine and extrapolated.

The look on her face said, "You're full of it." She was smart, if not overly literary. I took her book, opened it to the guillotine scene, and read it to her.

"They cut his *head* off?"

"Yop."

"How can *that* be a far, far better thing than anything else?"

I shrugged, then said, "You live in South Jamaica?"

"Yes. Where do you live?"

"Near Cunningham Park."

"You're on the wrong bus."

I shrugged again and said, "I bet you hate going to the swim meets."

"I bet you do too. What are you doing there anyway?"

"I'm a reporter for *The Hilltopper.*"

She stifled a yawn.

I followed her off the bus at some intersection on the outskirts of South Jamaica. We stood on the corner for a moment, as I looked off in both directions, no idea where I was. It had gotten colder, and either she took pity on me or she had planned this from the moment she had looked at me from the top of the pyramid—I'd like to believe it was the latter—but she invited me to her house for a hot chocolate.

Hands burrowed in my windbreaker, I followed her down two blocks of ramshackle wood-frame houses, with cheap aluminum siding and screened-in front porches.

Her house was a dull green with flaking white trim. She let us in the side door with her key and turned on the light, revealing an off-yellow kitchen with Formica counters and checkered linoleum.

It was obvious that there was no mother living in this house. This was not a kitchen that any self-respecting mother of that era would have operated in.

"Where's your mother?" I asked, stupidly, even though I knew the answer.

"She died."

"Oh. You live with your father?"

"Uh-huh. He works in the Brooklyn Navy Yard. He's a stevedore."

The image of the Polish stevedore with his grappling hook was never far from my mind during the maddening time I spent with Karen Szbachevsky. It hung over me like a sword of Damocles, threatening our stolen moments with real menace.

She took off her pea coat, threw it over a chair, then rattled around the kitchen in her cheerleading uniform. I watched her go to the refrigerator, take out a bottle of milk, pour it into a pot, sprinkle some Nesquik into the milk, and stir it.

She overcooked the hot chocolate, scalding the milk. It tasted awful. I drank the whole cup. When we were finished, I looked at her, struggling for something to say. Any port in the storm. She was no help. She just sat there looking bored.

Finally, I said, "Maybe I should be going."

"Okay."

I got up.

"Thanks for the hot chocolate."

"Sure."

She wasn't begging me to stay. The truth was I had boxed myself into a corner by getting up. There were only two things to do now—leave or try to kiss her. But my legs refused to move in her direction. So I asked her where the bus stop was going west and she told me.

I walked out the door, heard it close and lock behind me, walked half a block, getting progressively more pissed at myself. Why had I followed her down the hill in the first place? I had taken a bad bus into a bad part of town and gotten a scalded hot chocolate for my trouble.

It took me over an hour to get home. I went upstairs to my room, sat down at my desk, opened my school bag, and took out my notes on the John Adams meet. But I couldn't write a word. I thought about the girl with the ponytail and decided I couldn't live without her.

* * *

The next home meet was two weeks away. There was no way I was going to make it until then without seeing her, but I had no clear idea how to find her or, for that matter, what I would do when I did see her again. We weren't in any of the same classes, and the school was large enough that there were four different lunch periods. I had already used the wrong-bus gambit.

One of the Blumenthal twins, I could never tell which one, was in my plane geometry class. She was a complete airhead. She sat with a petrified expression on her face as Mr. Woodhouse explained the difference between an isosceles and an equilateral triangle. I stationed myself at the next desk and let her copy my proof on a quiz. I figured that had to be worth something.

"Thanks," she said breathily after the class was over. She gave me a penetrating look, a look that seemed to propose a little tit for tat. I asked her if she had a phone number for Karen Szbachevsky. "I have to interview her for *The Hilltopper*," I said. "We're doing an article on the cheerleaders."

"You can interview me," the Blumenthal twin said.

"Well . . ."

"After school today?"

"Uh . . ."

"At my house."

"Okay . . ."

At 3:45 I showed up at the twins' house with my reporter's note-book. Unlike Karen Szbachevsky, the Blumenthals lived on a good bus line, in a neighborhood called Jamaica Estates. The streets had English names, like Aberdeen Road or Chevy Chase Drive or Mid-land Parkway. I got off at Tudor Road and walked down a street lined with large faux Tudor houses, beveled glass windows, and thick bushy shrubs.

Either Bobbi or Sandi came to the door. She was wearing her cheerleading uniform, so I assumed it was the right one. She of-fered me a Nehi orange soda, grabbed a package of large pretzel sticks, and led me upstairs to her room.

The room was as large as my parents' living room. There were Ja-maica High School pennants on the wall, pictures of the basketball team, cheerleading trophies, a framed photo of Harry Belafonte, a plaque from the Future Nurses Club.

She plopped herself down on a blue taffeta bedspread that covered a capacious bed, took out a pretzel stick, and started nibbling at it.

"Okay," she said, "I'm ready."

I lurched forward. "How long have you been a cheerleader?"

"Since freshman year."

"Do you like it?"

"Of course. Why do you think I do it, silly?"

"What's it like?"

"You go to games and you cheer."

It started to get very warm in the room. I was alone with one of the Blumenthals in her bedroom; she was in a cheerleading skirt that had ridden halfway up her thighs sucking on pretzel sticks. There was blood flowing in different directions at the same time. I persevered.

"Is it hard to make the team?"

"I don't know. I just went to the tryouts and got picked."

I was racking my brains for something else to ask her when suddenly she asked, "You want to see them?"

"Huh?"

"You want to see my boobs?"

To be honest with you, I really didn't want to see them right at that moment. But it seemed like a difficult request to refuse. I mean, on what grounds do you refuse a request like that?

"What about the interview?" I stammered, but it was too late. She was already lifting her Jamaica High School sweater over her head, exposing a white Maidenform full to the brim.

"Pretty nice, huh?"

I nodded furiously.

"I'm not going to take the bra off, though. I don't do that for boys."

I shifted my weight to the other foot. She lowered her sweater.

"So what else do you want to ask me?"

"Karen Szbachevsky's phone number."

"I don't know. I just see her at practice. Anyway, she lives in South Jamaica, so I would never go there."

"Maybe I should be going."

"What about the rest of the interview?"

"I think I got the main points," I said and headed for the door.

On the stairway down, who do I run into but the other twin, on her way up.

"I was just doing an interview with your sister about cheerleading," I explained.

"Did she show you her boobs?"

"Yeah." I blushed and headed downstairs.

"Mine are better," she called after me.

* * *

That night I was up in my room slogging through Dickens when my mother yelled upstairs to tell me I had a phone call. I went into my parents' bedroom and picked up the phone.

"All you had to do was ask me and I would have given it to you," said Karen Szbachevsky.

"I didn't want to bother you."

"If you didn't want to bother me, why did you want my phone number?"

"I'm doing this interview about cheerleading for the paper . . ."

There was a long, breathy silence, then she said, "You could come over for a hot chocolate tomorrow after school. If you want."

"Okay."

"I'll meet you at the bus stop at a quarter to four."

* * *

She was ten minutes late. It was raining, and I stood under the awning of a pawnshop and waited for her. The first thing she said when she arrived, her loose-leaf notebook over her head, was, "You don't have an umbrella?"

I shook my head. What kind of self-respecting fifteen-year-old boy shows up at high school with an umbrella?

"How's *A Tale of Two Cities* going?" I asked.

"I'm not reading it anymore."

"How come?"

"I know what happens."

The bus arrived. We rode it not saying much, sitting side by side and watching the water stream down the overheated bus windows.

Even though we ran all the way from the bus stop to her house we were wet by the time she unlocked the side door and let us in. She took off her coat and shoes, and, padding around the kitchen in her socks, she poured the milk and the Nesquik into the pot and put it on the stove over a high fire.

Once again the milk was scalded. We sat on stools at the Formica bar drinking the hot chocolate, having a conversation in fits and starts.

When we finished our hot chocolates, we had arrived again at that moment when something had to happen. This time, I had promised myself, I would make my move. I was contemplating just how to approach, where I would put my hands, and whether I wanted her standing up or on the stool when she said, "So, you want to kiss me?" It was very matter-of-fact, as if she were saying, "You want another cup of hot chocolate?"

I got off the stool and moved toward her, making my way around the bar to her side. She got up to meet me. In her socks she came up to my nose.

She stood up on her tiptoes, and we mingled our hot-chocolate breath. Her eyes were closed. I left mine open and watched her eyes.

When we came up for air, we were both unsteady on our feet. We stood for a moment, shuffling our feet, then we sat back down. The kiss didn't seem to have resolved anything. We were back where we were before, separated by three feet of Formica, both a little dizzy.

"So how was it?" she asked.

"Great."

"I thought it was okay. I could have gone on longer."

"Me too."

The phone rang. She spoke in monosyllables, then hung up and said, "You have to go. My father's coming home early and I have to cook dinner."

I got up and she handed me my wet coat. "We could do better," she said.

"Yeah," I agreed.

"Tomorrow?"

"Sure."

*   *   *

And so began a series of after-school hot-chocolate and necking sessions. We did get progressively better. For one thing we stopped doing it standing up in the kitchen under the pitiless glare of the fluorescent light. We moved to the living room couch and dispensed with the hot chocolate.

It took a while to get to second base. But I eventually got there, after having my hand brushed away over and over as it inched its way down from her shoulder. It was two steps forward, one step back. By the time I slouched off to the bus stop late every afternoon, I could barely walk.

I had to lie through my teeth to my mother. I told her I had joined the Chess Club, and that it met after school every day. She started calling me the chess master. My father challenged me to a game and beat the shit out of me. "That must be some Chess Club you got there," he remarked.

The afternoon chess games with Karen Szbachevsky went on until Christmas vacation. I had to take a trip upstate to Rochester to visit my uncle Leonard and aunt Vera. My parents told everyone I was in the Chess Club. My twelve-year-old cousin Eugene mopped the floor with me.

We had to watch slides of their family trip the previous summer to the Canadian Rockies. There was a lot of Ping-Pong and knock hockey. We went to Niagara Falls and froze our asses off standing in thin yellow rain slickers watching the water cascade down in torrents. Eugene kept asking me questions about sex and wanting to compare masturbation techniques. He told me he could do it both left- and right-handed.

I spent a lot of time during that vacation thinking about Karen Szbachevsky and what was going to happen next. I was now safely on second base, staring off at third base, only ninety feet away. I had never been to third base before, but I'd heard about it from my friends. It was a base you had to get to if you wanted to get home.

First day back at school, after the New Year, the Blumenthal twin in my geometry class leaned over to me and batted a lot of eyelash. We were doing trapezoids and she was completely lost.

"Could you help me with my homework after school? Please?"

"I have Chess Club."

"We could play chess first. Then we could do trapezoids."

I had a vision of her playing chess in her Maidenform.

"My sister needs help too. You could help both of us. *Please* . . ."

That vision immediately mutated into two visions.

I didn't reply immediately. Mr. Woodhouse came in and called the class to order. I did not, however, think that I had actually agreed to help them with trapezoids. But when I arrived at sixth-period lunch, the other twin accosted me to let me know how grateful she was that I was going to help them with trapezoids at their house after school.

Though I had no prearranged rendezvous with Karen Szbachevsky that afternoon—in fact, we hadn't spoken since the Friday before vacation—I felt that I ought to cover my bases, so to speak. So I went in search of her during lunch period and managed to find her coming out of study hall.

She was wearing a pleated plaid skirt and a turtleneck sweater. A surge of raw jealousy went through me. The sweater was obviously covering a collection of hickeys she had gotten necking with the entire swimming team while I was upstate discussing jerk-off techniques with my cousin Eugene.

"So are we going to have a hot chocolate this afternoon?" I asked.

"How can you? You're helping Bobbi and Sandi with math." And she turned on a dime and walked away. I watched her ponytail bounce lightly between her shoulder blades.

* * *

Both Blumenthals were waiting for me when I walked out the door of the school at 3:15 that afternoon. My friend Mikey Siegel's eyes almost popped out of his head when he saw me walk off with not one, but two Blumenthals.

I sat between them on the bus, inhaling the buttery fragrance of their baby-powdered bodies, the math book open in my lap. Instead of looking like a man en route to a banquet, I looked like a man en route to a guillotine. 'Tis a far, far better thing that I do . . .

This time we went up to the other twin's room, which was exactly like her sister's except that it was pink. We all three sat on the bed. There were no chairs. They did their homework on the bed. They did *everything* on the bed, Bobbi or Sandi informed me.

I launched into rectangles, with the idea of approaching trapezoids through the general class of four-sided geometric figures. They sat on either side of me on the pink taffeta bedspread, chewing on their pretzels, their collective breath befogging my concentration.

I was up to parallelograms when Bobbi or Sandi said, "We want you to do something for us."

"What?" I said, a little too eagerly.

"Well," said the other one, "we want you to tell us which one's are better."

"Which ones of what?"

"*You* know." She giggled.

I did. I knew exactly what they were talking about. I was way ahead of them.

They got up simultaneously, turned around and faced me, standing side by side five feet away. In one perfectly coordinated movement, as if they were doing a cheerleading maneuver, they lifted their matching pink and blue sweaters over their heads.

I was staring at twin Maidenforms. They stood, hands by their sides, faces expectant, as if the answer to their question was completely obvious.

I have to tell you, I don't think anybody could have made that judgment. Even now, with some frame of reference, I wouldn't be able to tell you. They were perfect, all four of them. There was simply no choosing between them.

"Well?" They crossed their arms in front of them, below their bras, in a gesture of some impatience.

"They're both, I mean, all of them, are great."

The sisters frowned simultaneously. They were not happy with ambiguity. They needed to have a winner declared. They looked at each other, communicating in that silent language that twins use, and once again, in a single perfectly in coordinated movement, their hands went behind their backs and undid their bra snaps. Then, holding the two bras in their outside hands, they stood before me in all their splendor.

There is something about being five feet away from four perfect breasts when you're fifteen that is ultimately anticlimactic. This is a moment, believe me, that could never live up to its equivalent fantasy. And to make matters worse, they started to count in unison.

"One . . . two . . . three . . . four. . . ."

At the count of ten, they both said, at the exact same moment, "Which one?"

Being right-handed, I pointed blindly to the right. And as soon as I did, I regretted it. I saw the look on the other one's face, and it was a look that I would never want to see again on any woman's face.

By then, trapezoids seemed entirely beside the point, so I excused myself and headed for the door. They didn't ask me to stay.

*   *   *

The Blumenthal twins' geometry lesson would prove to be costly. Karen Szbachevsky must have found out about it because she started to avoid me. I looked for her at sixth-period study hall, but she wasn't there. I tried calling her, but I got the stevedore, who was less than cordial on the phone.

I didn't see Karen Szbachevsky again till the swim meet with Jackson Heights the following week. She was back on top of the pyramid, stepping on the starter. I placed myself in the optimal position for eye contact, and when we connected, there was something in her look that I interpreted as forgiveness.

So I waited for her at the bus stop on Hillside Avenue. When she showed up, she didn't say much, but she didn't discourage me from getting on the bus with her. I prattled away about my geeky cousin from Rochester, and she didn't tell me to shut up.

Nor did she say anything when I got off the bus with her. We walked the block and a half to the green house in silence. Thirty seconds later we were on the uncomfortable mohair couch in the dark living room.

The price I was going to pay, it turned out, was to be sent back to first base. It took me another week to regain second. There were some long hours on that couch getting my hand slapped away, but when I finally slipped it under the bra strap in back, my fingers remembered how to do the one-hand snap maneuver that I had mastered before Christmas vacation.

She had some sort of automatic timer inside her that told her when it was time to stop. And it was invariably at the moment I was thinking of making a mad dash for third base, that she wiggled free, got up, smoothed her skirt, and said that I'd better go. Before her father came home.

The mention of her father always sufficed to discourage any appeal from me to keep going.

We went on like this for the rest of January and most of February. My grades were slipping. My journalism apparently was too, because the editor, a snotty senior named Wendall White, threatened to take me off swimming and put me on lacrosse.

By the first week of March, I was still hovering between second and third base. Though I was taking a bigger and bigger lead off second, I wasn't any closer to third than I had been before Christmas vacation.

On a false spring day in early March, however, that would change. It was warm enough not to wear coats to school. She was wearing just a cardigan over her blouse, a thin white number with a ruffled collar. By this time I not only knew her wardrobe well but was familiar with the strategic difficulties each piece of clothing presented. This blouse buttoned down all the way to her waist, which made it easier to remove. The skirt she was wearing, though, was problematic. It was tighter than most of her skirts, which made forays underneath the hem difficult.

She seemed to be in a good mood on the bus, laughing at some of my stupider jokes and sticking her chewing gum on my nose. As soon as we got to her house, we went right at it.

I had the shirt and bra off in fifteen minutes, and, without breaking stride, I rounded second and headed for third. It must have been the weather. I had never moved that quickly.

Instead of trying to get under the skirt, I went for the zipper. I slid it down very slowly, fully expecting to get my hand grabbed and turned away. As each millimeter of the zipper released and nothing happened, I got bolder.

When the zipper was all the way down, I paused, to catch my breath and consider my next move. If I stopped now, this would become an accepted position. If I moved forward, however, I could carve out a whole new beachhead, or even get to third. Standing up.

It was at that point that Darwin kicked in and resolved the dilemma. It was my task on earth, though I didn't know it yet, to repopulate the species. This wasn't a decision. It was an evolutionary imperative.

So I moved forward, putting my hand on her hip and then slipping two fingers tentatively beneath the top of the skirt. My lips were getting bruised, but I didn't remove them in case she opened her eyes and realized what was happening. It will give you some idea how dumb I was that I thought that she didn't know what was happening.

The trip across her hip was tenuous. I fully expected to be stopped, my hand yanked away, perhaps even my face slapped. But she didn't do anything but continue to kiss me with her eyes closed. If you could call it kissing at this point.

I continued to proceed downward my hand inside her Fruit Of The Looms, my heart beating, until I reached a point at which a technical problem presented itself. Unless I wanted to sprain my wrist, I wasn't going to be able to reach the base.

Without breaking lip contact, she swiveled her hips to give me a better target. While she did this, she started to moan softly. I stumbled on, feeling the first strand of her finely spun pubic hair, another milestone. But you don't get a base for that.

By now she was moaning more audibly and thrusting her hips upward toward me. I got the point. I wasn't that dumb. I let my finger move down between her legs and slide, finally, into the moistness of third base.

I wish I could tell you that I was transported to heaven. Frankly, I wasn't. I knew absolutely nothing about this mysterious place and even less about what to do once I got there. As it turned out, it didn't seem to make a difference because she seemed to know exactly what to do.

She began moving against my finger, rising and falling in some sort of crazy Apache dance. Her lips left my lips and dug into my neck. As the movements increased in intensity, her thighs closed around my hand.

The next thing I remember is the feel of her teeth in my neck just before her whole body convulsed as if an electric current shot through her. And then, after a series of aftershocks, she went limp in my arms, her face buried in my neck.

We lay there for some time before I realized she was crying.

I said something stupid like, "Are you okay?"

She didn't answer. She cried for a while and then drifted off. I stayed where I was until a cramp in my arm got seriously painful. Gingerly, I extricated myself and got up.

I didn't know what else to do, so I left. All the way home I kept my finger enclosed in my fist. I went directly upstairs and into the bathroom, where I unwound my fist and stared at my finger. It didn't look any different.

Karen Szbachevsky wasn't in school the next day, or the day after that. I tried calling her after school. I got the stevedore. At 4:00 in the afternoon. He told me not to call there ever again and hung up.

It was one of the Blumenthals who informed me, a few days later, that Karen Szbachevsky was moving to Brooklyn. The other one said, with a nasty little smile on her face, that her father discovered she was screwing around in the afternoons and took her out of school.

"He came home and found her on the couch with her skirt unzipped. All the way."

"It's a good thing the guy wasn't there, or he would be dead now."

That afternoon I walked home instead of taking the bus. It was another false spring day with a warm, wet breeze in the air. I congratulated myself on not being dead, and on finally getting to third base, but it was without real conviction. The victory felt hollow.

Though I avoided washing my finger for a while, Karen Szbachevsky eventually evaporated. But slowly. For a long time afterward I remembered the bus rides, the hot chocolates, the feel of the mohair couch, and the way her lips pressed hard against mine. And I remembered that afternoon when I had slid fiercely into third.

That summer I finally made it home. Three weeks after my sixteenth birthday I crossed home plate with a chubby, drunk, nineteen-year-old waitress named Blanche in the back of her Rambler convertible. It was a deep disappointment.

*   *   *

This story has a epilogue. About ten years later I was living in a sublet in the Village and trying to make a living as a freelance writer. One night, I had some friends over, and we were smoking a joint and listening to Dylan. *Blonde on Blonde.* The doorbell rang.

When I saw Bobbi or Sandi Blumenthal standing there, I figured I was more stoned than I'd realized. She told me she had gotten the address from my mother and asked me if she could come in for a moment. I invited her in but avoided introducing her to my friends because I wasn't sure which twin I was dealing with.

She asked if there was a place we could be alone for a minute. I took her to the kitchen, and she closed the door behind us. She immediately took off her coat and unbuttoned her blouse. While I stood there like the stoned doofus that I was, she unsnapped her bra, showed me a pair of very substantial breasts, and asked me what I thought of them.

"Terrific," I said, or words to that effect.

"Have you ever seen any better ones?"

I shook my head as fast as I could.

"There aren't any," she said proudly before getting re-dressed and walking out of my apartment without saying another word.

Must have been the one on the left, I said to myself, and walked back out to smoke another joint.

III
MARGARET MEAD[9] AND THE
VOLLEYBALL EFFECT

The first time I saw Karen Myers she was naked. It was in Pennsylvania during the summer between my sophomore and junior years at college. She was perfectly tanned, with no bikini marks, and was serving a volleyball.

Watching her serve gave you some indication of what you were in store for. It would be a low, hard smash, barely clearing the net, the kind that you hit back, if you hit it back at all, as a big floating grapefruit that she would proceed to ram back down your throat. Then she would stand there, hands on hips, and smile at you fetchingly.

Risking hyperbole, I would say about Karen Myers naked that it didn't get any better. By any objective standard, if there is such a thing for naked women, she was in the 100th percentile.

Nude volleyball was the signature sport of the Sunnydell Ranch,[10] in Clarenceburg,[11] Pennsylvania. It was featured on the cover of its brochures, mailed in a plain brown wrapper, and in its ads in the back of nudist magazines. It was a coed noncontact sport, the perfect activity for a nudist camp or, as they preferred to call themselves, a naturist resort.

[9]Short, chubby anthropologist (1901–1978) and author of *Coming of Age in Samoa*.
[10]Not its real name.
[11]Not a real place.

The Sunnydell Ranch was not a ranch, though it had pretensions of being one. There wasn't a horse or a cowboy anywhere on its "twelve acres nestled in the foothills of the Poconos." Pam and Wally, the couple who ran the place, gave things ranchy names and called everybody *partner.*

"Howdy, partner," they would say to you in their lacquered New Jersey drawls, their sun-dried skin hanging off them like leatherette upholstery.

I was working as a waiter in the dining room, trying to earn money to help pay my tuition at the sub–Ivy League college I was attending. In addition to my $115-a-week salary, I got room and board, such as they were, and all the naked women I could look at.

Let me tell you the truth right off: The law of diminishing returns applies just as well to nudity as it does to bushels of wheat. Seeing all that succulent flesh serving volleyballs, lounging beside the pool or, in my case, sitting and eating corn on the cob with a napkin in the lap, quickly becomes not only quotidian but antierotic. You soon begin to fantasize how people look with their clothes *on.*

Staff members were encouraged to take their clothes off as well. Pam and Wally believed that nakedness was a spiritual state. They gave talks about the transcendental quality of naturism at night in the Bunkhouse—a sort of combination social hall and rec room featuring a Ping-Pong table, board games, paperback western novels, a record player, and a collection of Vaughn Monroe and Gene Autry 45's. It was, according to Wally, easier to become One with Nature bare-assed than in clothes.

There were two major no-no's at the ranch: sitting down anywhere without first putting a towel underneath you, and public sexual contact. And it went without saying, of course, that any public tumescence was also strictly verboten. Believe me, it's the last thing that happens to you in a nudist camp.

When I tell men that I spent time in a nudist camp, it's always the first question they ask me. And I always tell them the same thing. You don't get one. Take my word for it. Besides the fact that most people, Karen Myers notwithstanding, look better in their clothes than out of them, there is something inherently detumescent about volleyball, archery, Ping-Pong, and the other noncontact sports that are big among the naturists. Call it the Volleyball Effect.

Nevertheless, I wore a bathing suit and an apron in the Chuck Wagon, the knotty-pine dining room with green plastic chairs and a large portrait of Roy Rogers and Dale Evans, fully clothed. I considered it an occupational safety measure. We were carrying hot soup; the cook was half Japanese, half Cherokee, hit the sauce, and seemed very cavalier about the way he used knives.

Karen Myers came to the Sunnydell Ranch with her parents, Arthur and Phyllis, two anthropologists who taught at Columbia and had, apparently, each published seminal books in their field. They were in their late forties, thin, with the nervous, graceless energy of hard-core intellectuals. Arthur would sit by the pool, his schlong hanging nonchalantly on his thigh, reading books in German and smoking a white briar pipe. On one side of him would be his wife, Phyllis, a washcloth over each nipple to keep them from getting sunburned, reading books in French; on the other side would be his daughter, Karen, reading Erich Fromm.[12]

In the Chuck Wagon Karen Myers would occasionally flash me a generic smile while I served her her daily tuna salad and iced tea. But we didn't really have a conversation until the night I wandered

[12]Enormously popular psychoanalyst, whose book *The Art of Loving,* a tour de force of reductive heuristics, was a best-seller in the 1960s.

into the Bunkhouse to get something to read. There were a bunch of Zane Grey and Louis L'Amour novels on the bookshelf, and I was looking through them trying to decide which one I didn't want to read the least when she walked in with her parents. Even though I had been working there for two months, it was still weird for me to see naked people indoors at night.

Arthur invited me to play doubles Ping-Pong with them, guys against girls. I was wearing jeans and a T-shirt. It felt a little unseemly to me to play Ping-Pong with three naked people, but Arthur already had a paddle in my hand and was volleying for serve.

Under the best of circumstances, which this wasn't, I am not a very good Ping-Pong player. I have underdeveloped hand-eye coordination. I didn't play tennis or bowl, and I was a marginal waiter. I was particularly unspectacular that night.

It turned out that Phyllis wasn't much of a player either, so it was essentially a match between Arthur and his daughter. They went after each other viciously, slicing and slamming with abandon. They won.

Arthur invited me back to their cabin for a cup of herbal tea after the Ping-Pong.

"I'm not really dressed for it," I said, with a stab at irony.

"That's all right with us," he answered, with no discernible sense of humor.

Their cabin, called the Ponderosa, had rough-hewn wooden furniture, a bear rug, a nonfunctional fireplace, and a Lava lamp. There was one bedroom. Karen Myers presumably slept on the foldout couch. We sat around the oak coffee table, sipping hibiscus tea as Arthur talked about a certain South Pacific tribe in which women bit their husbands' penises on their wedding night as a sign of their devotion. When he saw me wince, he explained that they only bit the surface to draw a little blood.

Karen Myers was majoring in social anthropology. I asked her what that was, and she told me. But I was hardly listening. Now that we were no longer playing Ping-Pong under a fluorescent bulb but sitting close together in the low light of the Lava lamp, with Karen sprawled out casually on the couch, the Volleyball Effect was wearing off.

As she went on talking, she shifted her posture with an apparent lack of self-consciousness. But I'm convinced she knew exactly what she was doing. As I was to learn, Karen Myers always knew exactly what she was doing.

Eventually her parents excused themselves to go to bed.

"Don't get up," Arthur said, as he wished me good night. If he'd had an ounce of wit, the remark would have been very funny. They disappeared into their bedroom, closing the door behind them and leaving me alone with their beautiful young naked social-anthropologist daughter.

She reached for a macramé bag, in which she rummaged around for a plasticine envelope, a pack of rolling papers, and a lighter. Then she rolled the tightest joint I had even seen.

"Are you self-conscious about your body?" she asked me.

"Not at all," I lied.

"So why do you walk around with your clothes on at a nudist camp?"

"I don't know. . . . I guess I just like to be different. I mean, if everyone were wearing clothes, I would probably be naked."

"What if I got dressed now? Would you take off your clothes?"

She lit the joint, inhaled deeply, passed it to me. As I took a hit, she said, "Are you embarrassed because you have an erection?"

I shook my head quickly, holding in the smoke.

"Believe me, I've seen my share of erections."

"I don't doubt it."

"It's the great equalizer," she went on. "Women spend their lives as sexual objects. But when you're naked it's the reverse. It's the men who are self-conscious. You have to walk around trying to hide your feelings. Why hide them? They're just an example of polymorphous perversity. The body is full of sexual energy that just gets repressed, which causes all sorts of somatic problems, not to mention antisocial activity . . ."

As we smoked the joint, the conversation became more abstract. Terms like *polymorphous perversity* tend to bring the Volleyball Effect back. The fact was that, gorgeous and naked as she might be, she was boring me to death.

I decided to make a run for it. I stood up, now completely volleyballed, and faced her.

"I got to be up at six for breakfast setup."

The grass had made her eyes big. You could have driven a truck through her pupils. One of her hands was absently playing with a nipple. Her eyes drifted down to check out if anything was going on, and when she saw that there was nothing happening, she looked hurt.

The Chief was up and loaded when I got back to the dormitory.

"You fuck her?"

"Who?"

"Whad'ya mean *who*? that gorgeous quim with the pink nipples I been jerking off to since she got here that's who Frimmer says you was playing Ping-Pong with her where'd you do her under the table what was she like tell me?"

"Go to sleep, Chief."

"I can't go to no fucking sleep thinking about her pussy was it wet how many times did you do it where'd you stick it in did she like it I bet she screamed holy motherfucker didn't she?"

*   *   *

Hell apparently had no fury because she didn't even look at me when I served her her French toast the next morning. It was foggy and damp, and she was wearing a shirt in the Chuck Wagon. I can't begin to tell you how much sexier she looked in an open man-tailored shirt, than she looked stark naked.

But the sun burned off the fog by eleven, and she was back bare-assed on the volleyball court kicking ass. As I was gazing across the volleyball court at her in the distance, I was accosted by a middle-aged wholesale furniture dealer named Murray. Murray flew up from Bucks County for weekends in his own small plane.

"God threw out the mold after He made her," he said, standing beside me and watching Karen Myers serve a winner. "I'd like to take her up in my plane, but I don't trust myself."

"Just get her to talk about anthropology, and you'll be fine."

*   *   *

One afternoon a few days later, Wally asked me to clear away some of the glasses from the poolside. You didn't say no to Wally, and so I went down to the pool and started gathering glasses. There were a couple of the old Germans sitting around playing pinochle, a mother with her two deeply tanned children, and a flabby Motor Vehicle Department clerk from Paramus, whose stomach completely obscured his genitals. I didn't realize Karen Myers was there as well until she broke the surface of the pool and swam over to the side.

"You look pretty stupid in those jeans," she said.

She was leaning her elbows up against the coping of the pool, water glistening off her body. I realized that the Chief had been right. Her nipples were the shade of pink you see on early spring roses.

"Want to go for a hike?" she asked.

"A hike?"

"Yeah. There's a bunch of walking trails on the other side of the lake." She saw me hesitate and added, "It's all right. You can wear your clothes."

When she showed up at the head of the trail, she was wearing socks and sneakers. And that was it.

It was hot, and I took off my T-shirt and tucked it into my jeans. We skirted the edge of the lake and headed up one of the paths. As we walked she told me about a trip she had taken with her parents to New Guinea when she was sixteen. The headman of the very primitive tribe they were studying offered her father ten women, a straw hut, three goats, and his best blow dart if he could have her.

"Wow," I said and meant it. "What did he say?"

"He said it was my decision."

"C'mon, really? You were only sixteen."

"So? I wasn't a virgin. It would have been interesting from an anthropological point of view."

I hesitated, not sure I wanted to know the answer to the next question, but my curiosity got the best of me. "So . . . did you do it?"

She shook her head.

"How come?"

"He had really bad teeth."

At the top of the trail, there was a small, shaded pond in a clearing of scrub oak and willow trees. We were both sweating heavily by then, and without a word she took off her sneakers and socks and jumped into the pond.

"Come on," she said. "Don't be such a drag."

I was out of excuses. As if I really wanted one at that point. I took off my shoes, slipped out of my jeans and boxers, and went in after her.

The water was clear and cool. There was a view all the way back to the camp; in the distance you could see the Chuck Wagon and the Bunkhouse, looking like miniature models in an architectural sketch.

I closed my eyes and savored the feeling of the cold water against my skin. It was a moment of calmness and clarity, a moment of detachment from the here and now. I floated on the water, cool and detached, until I felt her against my back. She put one hand on my shoulder, as the other one reached around in front and found what she was looking for. In spite of the cold water, I grew very quickly in her hand.

I swiveled around to face her, and we kissed. It was a very sweet kiss, considering that she had her hand around my dick.

I remember wondering how many times in my life I could expect to find myself skinny-dipping in a clear pond at the top of a mountain with a woman whose mold God threw out after He used it.

I wish I could remember more of what happened in that pond. I wish I could remember the salty taste of her neck, the cool tightness of her skin against me, the way the goose bumps popped up, the crazy little-girl whimpering and the grating of her nails; I wish I could remember how she locked her thighs around me like a tourniquet and nearly squeezed me to death, how we got out of the pond and dried off in the hot sun without saying a word.

By the time we made it down the mountain and reentered the camp, life returned to normal. But it never really did return completely to normal. Nothing ever does.[13] I was now both blessed and cursed with a sense memory of her. The Volleyball Effect was no longer consistently operative.

*   *   *

From that time on we became insatiable. It took a great deal of imagination to find places to do it that didn't involve a hot, sweaty forty-five-minute trek up a mountain. Our favorite place became the airport—a graded dirt strip, with one or two planes parked alongside.

One afternoon we were about to do it under the fuselage of Murray's single-engine Cessna, when Murray himself showed up.

"You want to go up for a spin?" he asked us. "The countryside's beautiful around here. We can fly over the Delaware Water Gap."

Though I didn't have a pressing need to see the Delaware Water Gap from the air, I figured why not. Karen Myers and I had just shared a joint by the lake, and it sounded like exactly the type of thing you wanted to do stoned on a hot summer afternoon.

The three of us climbed into Murray's Cessna, Karen Myers riding shotgun and me in the jump seat behind her sitting on the parachutes. Murray put on his pilot's hat and headset started up the engine, and filed his flight plan with Allentown airport.

The Cessna slid smoothly off the ground and flew low over the camp. Arthur and Phyllis were poolside with their books. Wally was patrolling in his cowboy hat. A volleyball game was in progress. All was well at the Sunnydell Ranch.

---

[13]Vide infra, the second law of thermodynamics, p. 148.

Murray banked the plane, and we gained altitude.

"Pretty spectacular, isn't it?" he exclaimed as he leveled the plane off.

"Uh-huh," we both replied, more or less simultaneously. While Karen Myers and I tripped on the scenery, Murray rambled on about what we were seeing down below. By the time we were approaching the Delaware Water Gap his voice had become part of the background noise, along with the engine, and I only noticed it when it stopped.

I looked over at Murray and saw him flipping switches on the dashboard.

"Something wrong?" I asked.

"I don't know," Murray responded, continuing to flip switches.

Karen Myers's head swiveled to face Murray. "There's something *wrong*?"

"My altimeter isn't reading correctly."

"What does that *mean*?"

"It means that I have no way of gauging our altitude."

"Can't you just look out the window and see how high we are?"

The phrase *how high we are* would have ordinarily sent Karen Myers and me into a new stoned giggle fit if it weren't for the fact that we were in a single-engine plane a few thousand feet in the air flown by a nudist named Murray. This was a moment when you wanted to see some gray-templed, square-jawed veteran of 61 million flight hours at the controls in a trim blue uniform and not a paunchy middle-aged man without his clothes.

"It could be nothing," Murray said.

Karen Myers and I nodded furiously, as if our nodding would corroborate what Murray had just said.

"But it could be trouble," he added.

"So what are you going *to do*?"

"We should probably make an emergency landing at Allentown . . ."

"Emergency landing?" We didn't like the sound of that at all.

Murray flipped some more switches and then spoke into his headphone, "Allentown, this is Cessna N549448 . . ."

So much for the Delaware Water Gap.

As we lowered altitude and prepared for our emergency landing, my young life flickered before me. I was both scared and angry. It seemed unfair to check out like this. I was only on my third Karen, and I was about to be splattered on the runway of the Allentown airport with two people I didn't really know that well because of a faulty altimeter.

I could already see the headline: THREE NUDISTS CRASH AT ALLENTOWN. Would they know that I wasn't a nudist? Would my reputation ever be cleared? Who would get them to print a retraction—ONE OF THE THREE PEOPLE INVOLVED IN THE FATAL SMALL PLANE CRASH AT ALLENTOWN AIRPORT WASN'T A NUDIST BUT IN FACT A WAITER WORKING HIS WAY THROUGH COLLEGE.

I kept closing my eyes, then opening them as Murray dropped altitude. I glanced over at Karen Myers, who was humming some mantra to herself and staring zombielike out the cockpit window.

Five minutes later we were on the ground.

It was a perfectly smooth landing. But the sight of the fire engines lining the side of the runway didn't make it seem very smooth. I was still feeling shaky as we taxied to a stop. I looked out the window and saw the emergency crew approaching the plane with their sirens blaring.

Murray was listening to the tower give him further emergency landing instructions. He said, "Roger," a few times, then, "Over and out." He turned to us and said, "They want us to deplane immediately."

I don't think it was until that moment that we remembered we weren't wearing any clothes. If there was ever a moment to laugh, it was then. But seeing all those men in their protective clothing carrying hoses and fire axes discouraged us.

My eyes went to the parachutes, but Murray immediately told me that they were designed not to be opened inside the plane.

"Well, I suppose we can ask them to toss up some blankets," Murray suggested.

"Fuck that," said Karen Myers. "There is nothing at all shameful about the human body. How do we get out of this thing?"

Murray hit a switch to open the cockpit hatch and lower the landing stairway.

From the ground, the emergency crew could see only our heads through the plane's windows. They had no idea what they were in store for.

"Shouldn't you go first?" I suggested to Murray.

"The captain's got to be the last person to abandon ship," he said, with perfect gravity, like it was Mutiny on the Fucking Bounty instead of three naked people in a Cessna at the Allentown airport.

Fed up with this equivocation, Karen Myers climbed over Murray, went down the stairs, and faced the firemen as if she were descending a grand staircase in an evening gown. She did it with perfect nonchalance. Imagine, if you will, Jacqueline Kennedy deplaning in Paris with the Oleg Cassini suit and the pillbox hat. The five men snapped to attention, raising their hoses and hatchets in tribute to the beautiful naked young woman arriving at their airport.

I came down the stairs next, a sarcastic grin on my face in an attempt to disassociate myself from the two card-carrying nudists—as if to say, "Hey, don't look at me—I just work there."

Someone went to get blankets. But, it being 88 degrees outside, it took a while to find them. In the meantime, there were a number of faces pressed against the glass of the passenger terminal.

Karen Myers stood proudly on display, without any self-consciousness, looking as if she were about to serve a volleyball. The firemen stood opposite her, trying both to avert their eyes and to sneak looks at the same time.

"What's the matter—you've never seen a naked woman before?"

It didn't take long to repair the altimeter, but the paperwork took forever. By that time, a couple of mobile news crews from Allentown had sped out to interview us. Wrapped in her blanket, Karen Myers delivered a tutorial on the health benefits of naturism and polymorphous perversity to the local reporters. I declined comment.

The sun was just setting when we got back to the ranch. We had been on the six o'clock news and were already celebrities. Wally had spoken to reporters on the phone, and though he expressed concern for our safety, you could tell he was wallowing in the free PR.

Arthur and Phyllis were fairly blasé about the fact that their daughter had had to make a naked emergency landing that afternoon. They appeared to be more concerned that their Scrabble game had been interrupted.

The Chief, of course, was anything but blasé.

"You iner going down?"

"What?"

"You iner to the hilt all the way touching her bottom making her scream bloody hell top of her lungs when the plane bailed fucking out of sight man?"

*   *   *

In the weeks that followed, Arthur and Phyllis were very cordial to me. They treated me like one of the family, inviting me for Parcheesi games at the Ponderosa in the evenings and Ping-Pong games in the Bunkhouse. I'm not sure whether they knew that I was having sex with their daughter, or cared.

One night, after her parents excused themselves to go to bed, Karen Myers convinced me to do it right there on the floor with her parents a few feet away behind the flimsy door.

"It'll be like Zen," she whispered, "smooth water over stone."

She was on top of me before I had a chance to say no. We started out slowly, the smooth water sliding very gently over the stone, but then things got progressively less Zen, and I had to keep my hand over her mouth to keep her from screaming.

If-we're-not-careful-we-can-get-caught sex became her new passion. She would sneak into the dormitory at two in the morning and insist on doing it with the Chief snoring a few feet away. We did it in the backseat of her parents' Volvo in broad daylight in the parking lot. We did it in the supply closet next to the kitchen. We did it, at night, on the porch of the Bunkhouse, with her sitting on my lap, while having a conversation with the half-blind old Germans.

By the time Labor Day rolled around, we had done it just about everywhere at the Sunnydell Ranch. Except in a bed. And it wasn't until we got back to the city that I saw her with her clothes on.

*   *   *

We had a date to go to dinner and a movie about a week after we returned to New York. I picked her up at the Myerses' apartment on West End Avenue in the Eighties.

Arthur answered the door, naked and smoking his white briar pipe. He led me into the apartment, where he introduced me to a half dozen middle-aged anthropologists sitting in the living room with cocktails in their hands. They too were naked.

"Please. Don't get up," I said, in all sincerity.

It didn't stop them. They all got up to shake my hand.

"Karen will be right out," Phyllis said. "Care for a daiquiri?"

I declined and sat on the edge of the couch as the anthropologists returned to their discussion of pre-Columbian courtship rituals.

Karen Myers appeared at last, breathtaking in a light sweater, toreador pants, and heels. We made our excuses to the naked anthropologists, who once again insisted on getting up and shaking hands.

I followed her to the elevator, already calculating how long it would take me to get her clothes off. On the way down, I said, "It must be weird having naked anthropologists around your house."

"I grew up with it."

"Who was the short fat woman?"

"Margaret Mead."

"I just saw Margaret Mead *nude*?"

"You and half the population of Samoa."

*   *   *

We ate in a mediocre Indian restaurant on Broadway, saw a mediocre Hungarian movie at the Thalia, and then took the IRT downtown to a friend's apartment I was borrowing on East Fifth Street.

I put "Sunshine Superman"[14] on the stereo, rolled a joint, and we smoked it down to a cinder. Then I did something I had never done before with Karen Myers. I took her clothes off.

[14]Song by the British rock star Donovan that went well with marijuana.

We made love on my bed. It was pretty pro forma. She must have felt the same way because the little cries were littler than they had ever been. She barely squeezed me with her thighs when we were finished.

We lay there staring at the water-stained ceiling. Upstairs the Puerto Rican cabdriver was screaming at his wife. Police sirens blared on Avenue B. The sink in the bathroom dripped loudly.

The Indian meal lay heavy on our stomachs. The Hungarian film lay heavy on our souls. Her throat was a little scratchy. She thought she might be coming down with a cold. I heard her gargling with Listerine in the bathroom.

We dressed without saying much. There was a tandoori sauce stain on her sweater.

It was drizzling when I walked her to First Avenue to get her a cab. We must have waited in the rain at least twenty minutes for a taxi.

"See you," I said when one finally arrived and I opened the door to help her in.

"Yeah," she replied and slid into the backseat.

"I'll call you," I promised, as she gave the driver her address.

I never did.

IV

EDUCATION SENTIMENTALE

*C*ara *is not Karen in Italian.* But it's close, only one syllable apart. And even if it weren't, Cara Boleri would merit a place among the Karens. A prominent place.

To this day certain silly Italian pop songs reduce me to tears. And I am unable to drink Chianti without choking up, or reread the following letter without going back to that spring in Rome in 1966 when I fell madly in love with her.

Caro mio . . .

I miss you, meany boy. I am so *triste. Molto triste.* I remember our *baci* (kises?). *Molti baci.* . . . *Cheri, je t'aime, cheri je t'adore, come la salsa di pomodore.* Remember the song on the Via Sistina, *quando* we make *l'amore* after lunch? *O, caro mio,* I am *triste.* Send me your heart . . . *ti voglio bene.* . . . Cara

If there were a way to have sent her my heart, believe me, I would have done it a long time ago. I keep this letter folded inside a copy of Dante Rossetti's[15] sonnets, along with some pictures of her.

There is one photograph in particular that brings back that intoxicating Roman spring I spent with her in particularly sharp focus.

[15]Melancholy English poet and painter (1828–1882), one of the founders of the Pre-Raphaelites, who, in a fit of grief, buried his wife, who had OD'd on laudanum, with a number of his poems, then changed his mind years later and had her body exhumed in order to recover the poems.

We are sitting, Cara Boleri and I, at an outdoor restaurant near the Piazza del Popolo, along with some friends—Tomás, the Filipino painter; his lover, Paco, the Brazilian nightclub dancer; and Giovanni, the slender young Italian law student with the bedroom eyes.

There are empty wine bottles on the table, crumbs, small coffee cups, cigarettes. Soon we will disperse for our siestas. Cara Boleri and I will go back on my Vespa to the narrow bed in the Pensione 88 on the Via Sistina and make love until the cool of the early evening.

What is striking about this photo is how sad she seems. The rest of us are smiling and jaded with too much food and wine, but she looks as if she had just sat through the last act of *La Traviata*. She carried her sadness around with her wherever she went.

I met her in late March of that year, on the tail end of an odyssey through Europe. The previous June I had graduated from my sub–Ivy League college with a degree, more or less by default, in English. I was not eager to go to graduate school and get another degree, since I didn't see any use for the one I already had, so I saved up a little money working as a busboy during the summer and took a cut-rate student boat to Europe in September.

After several months living on the cheap in London and Paris and a hitchhiking trip through France and Spain, I bought a Vespa for fifty-three dollars from a shitfaced sailor in Barcelona and took off across the Riviera for Italy.

I had the phone number in Rome of Giovanni Brazziani, a young Italian who had spent a year as an exchange student at my college in upstate New York. Giovanni was tall with fine, angular features and, already at twenty-one, thinning hair. He had grown up living all over the world with his diplomat father and had acquired a polish and sophistication around women that compared favorably to the frat-house, beer-swilling style of my contemporaries. It was no surprise that he enjoyed great success with the coeds of various women's colleges in the area.

Once at a fraternity party I asked him to what he attributed this success with women. He looked at me strangely, as if the question had no meaning to him. I tried to refine it but finally just simply asked him, "How come you get laid so much?"

"It is of no consequence to, as you say, get laid," he replied. "You must love a woman completely. So much so that when you say good-bye to her, your heart aches."

This was advice that had very little resonance for a twenty-one-year-old American who had grown up with the street wisdom that sex was some sort of combination of track meet and hunt. I credit Giovanni and that year in Europe for teaching me just how defective my sexual education had been.

*   *   *

Anyway, by the time I arrived in Rome in late March, chilled and weary from a thousand kilometers across southern France and northern Italy on a motor scooter, I had very little real knowledge of women and even less money. I called Giovanni and asked if he could suggest a cheap hotel or youth hostel.

"You must come stay with us," he said.

An hour later I was sitting, in my jeans and least dirty shirt, sipping a glass of Pinot Grigio, in the elegantly furnished living room of Signor and Signora Brazziani's commodious apartment near the Villa Borghese.

Brazziani *père* was nearly completely bald and looked like Francisco Franco.[16] La Signora was tall and thin, like her son, and glided

[16]Hair-challenged Spanish dictator (1892–1975).

ethereally across the exquisite carpet. Giovanni, relaxed and elegant
as ever, was wearing a cashmere sweater, very thin linen slacks, and
leather loafers soft enough to fold up into your pocket.

As I sat listening to Signor Brazziani talk about his recent trip to
Rio de Janeiro, my eyes kept landing on a lovely young woman,
with dark hair and dark eyes, who sat quietly on an easy chair, her
shoes off, looking dreamily over her glass of sherry. She was introduced to me as Cara Boleri, a friend of Giovanni.

At dinner I was seated directly across from her. We ate the most
tender veal I'd ever tasted, and spoke about things I no longer remember. I couldn't keep my eyes off her.

Signor Brazziani must have noticed my preoccupation because
he remarked that the women of Rome were the most beautiful
women in the world. His eyes growing cloudier with each glass of
wine, he waxed poetic, "You must experience our Roman women,
but I must warn you to be careful. If you drink too much at the
fountain you will be their slave forever."

It wasn't clear to me if this was an encouragement or a caution.
As it turned out, it was a little of both.

After dinner Giovanni suggested we go for a walk in the Villa
Borghese, he, Cara Boleri, and I. She smiled at him, one of her rare,
and therefore especially precious, smiles, and we went.

And that's when it began—that night in late March in the Villa
Borghese, as we walked under a gauzy moon inhaling the aroma of
semitropical vegetation. The three of us strolled hand in hand, with
Cara Boleri in the middle, through the old park, mostly deserted at
this hour except for the occasional well-dressed prostitute smoking
under a streetlamp.

Giovanni described the exotic plants and the pigeon-speckled
statues. Cara Boleri listened intently, occasionally saying something
in Italian to Giovanni.

After we had been walking for a half hour or so, we stopped to admire a statue that, Giovanni explained, was done by a disciple of Bernini. It was of a satyr disporting with a nymph. He looked like he was having a good time. Maybe it was the statue, maybe it was the wine and the veal piccata, maybe it was the fragrance of Cara Boleri's perfume, a sort of musty lilac, but I had the distinct impression she was squeezing my hand.

Standing there under the lambent haze of the yellow lamp, I felt a soft but nonetheless palpable pressure on my fingers. It was just subtle enough to make me question whether it wasn't anything more than a reflex muscle spasm.

I had no idea what to make of this. She kept her eyes straight ahead as Giovanni spoke, giving no indication that she was doing anything but listening to him.

When we got back to the Brazzianis' apartment building, Giovanni asked me if I would mind running Cara Boleri back home on my Vespa. His father's car, he explained, was in the shop for repairs, and he himself had never learned to drive a motor scooter.

I would have driven her to Sicily without having to be asked twice. So I kick-started the Vespa and, after kissing Giovanni on both cheeks, Cara Boleri climbed on sidesaddle[17] and we took off together up the Via del Corso.

She was staying on the Via Appia Antica, the old Roman road on the outskirts of the city. Her arms around my waist, her face a few inches from my left ear, her Chianti-tinted breath warm on my neck, she whispered directions in her throaty, strangely inflected voice.

We drove past the baroque birthday cake dedicated to Victor Emmanuel, then past the Colosseum, looking surreal in the

---

[17]Method used at that time by Italian women in tight skirts to mount motorcycles, which was condemned by the Vatican as sinful and by the carabinieri as a cause of traffic accidents.

shrouded moonlight. The night was redolent of spring and recent rain. Out on the Appia Antica were Roman ruins bathed in the hazy glow of a waxing moon. We drove for a long time before she told me to pull into a drive that led to an old villa behind a rusted gate.

We dismounted and stood for a moment outside the gate.

"You live here?"

She nodded and said, "I work as nanny for Belgium peoples. But I am free almost all evenings unless they go out, but they do not go out because they are uninteresting peoples."

That was the most she had said to me all evening.

"So you are free?"

"Most definitely. If you like it I can show you Roma."

. I nodded. I nodded for a long time before she reached up and touched my cheek, to stop me from nodding. I stopped nodding. Then, her hand still on my face, she reached up and kissed me. But not on two cheeks, as she had kissed Giovanni. No, this one was right on the money.

If you could keep one kiss in your life, in a wine cellar, to take out and taste whenever you felt like it, I would choose that kiss. It was as if I had never kissed a woman before. It was as if that kiss erased every other kiss I had gotten during the first twenty-one years of my life.

I drove back to Rome in a stupor. It was amazing that I didn't wrap the scooter around a lamppost.

I slept deeply and dreamlessly that night in a big canopied bed in the guest bedroom and awoke to coffee and croissants, served by a maid in a black uniform and a white apron.

"*Buon giorno*," she said, opening the heavy brocade drapes to let the day in. "*Che bella giornata.*"

The events of the previous night came back in one thrilling flush.

Did Cara Boleri really kiss me on the Via Appia Antica? Or was it just some crossed wire, some fragment of an Italian movie I had seen that was stuck in my subconscious? Had I stumbled into the middle of *L'Avventura?*[18] Was Cara Boleri actually Monica Vitti?[19]

There was a soft knock on the door.

"Entrez," I said in the wrong language. The door opened, and Giovanni entered.

"Good morning," he said, sitting down on an antique desk chair and indicating with his hand that I should start eating.

I buttered my croissant with rich soft butter and poured some coffee, avoiding his eyes.

"So," he said, "you saw the Appia Antica last night?"

I spilled some coffee as I nodded.

"In the moonlight," he continued.

"Uh-huh."

"Bellissimo, no?"

"Uh-huh."

"She has already telephoned this morning. You are to meet her at the top of the Spanish Steps at four o'clock. She will show you the Fontana di Trevi, you know, the fountain in which Anita Ekberg[20] bathed in *La Dolce Vita.*"[21]

"Are you going to be joining us?"

"No. I have a lecture to attend."

"Uh-huh."

"So, you are on your own."

---

[18]Slow-moving neo-realistic Italian film directed by Michelangelo Antonioni, in which a number of people wander around looking for a missing woman, who may or may not actually be missing.

[19]One of the wanderers.

[20]Swedish bombshell, whose films include *The Screaming Mimi, Call Me Bwana, Abbott and Costello Go to Mars,* and *War and Peace.*

[21]Federico Fellini's 1960 masterpiece, in which Marcello Mastroianni sits in cafés on the Via Veneto and people drive by in sports cars and say, *"Ciao,* Marcello."

There was a crinkly little smile around the edges of his mouth. It was his father's smile, a smile that had several layers to it.

* * *

The next four hours passed slowly. I tried, with little success, to read. I had been dragging a dog-eared copy of Camus's *La Peste*[22] around with me and hacking my way through it with my inadequate French. It was the kind of book I thought you looked good reading in a café.

There was still a good deal of sun in the sky at four o'clock. It was a cool day with a smart breeze coming off the Tiber. I found the Piazza di Spagna, climbed up the Spanish Steps, sat down on one side of the top step, and took out Camus.

Long minutes passed. The rats were multiplying in Oran. I looked over the top of the book, scanning the piazza below for her, my eyes gliding over the shifting sea of people. More minutes passed. The bells of Trinità dei Monti tolled 4:30, then a quarter to five.

I was beginning to despair. Maybe she missed her bus. Maybe the uninteresting Belgians got an unexpected invitation to a cocktail party.

And then she was there. I smelled her before I saw her. The musty lilac wafted into my nostrils a split second before I felt a pair of hands cover my eyes.

"Who is it?"

I told her. She let go and I turned around. I looked up at her, seeing her for the first time in daylight.

There are very few women whom raw unfiltered sunlight improves, who look better in broad daylight than in moonlight or in

---

[22]*The Plague*, allegorical work by the French novelist of North African descent (1913–1960), whose *Myth of Sisyphus* is the tale of a man who enjoys carrying a heavy ball up a hill only to have it roll down again as soon as he gets to the top.

the low warm lighting of a Roman apartment. The textured light brought out her exquisite skin tones, enriched her lips and eyes with color.

"*Ciao,*" she said, sitting down beside me and taking out a pack of Nazionales. She lit one, inhaled deeply. She offered no explanation for being nearly an hour late. She never would. At no point during our time together would Cara Boleri ever be on time for anything. Or ever explain why she wasn't.

"So," I said, "are we going to see the Trevi Fountain?"

She shrugged, exhaled, blowing out a thin stream of smoke. Then she got up, grabbed my hand, and said, "Come."

We walked down the steps, hand in hand. But we didn't go to the fountain. In the three and a half months I was in Rome I never saw the Trevi Fountain.

We walked through the piazza, past American Express, then down a narrow cobblestone side street until we turned into a courtyard. At the rear of the courtyard was an outdoor stairway that ascended into a parklike overgrown hillside.

The vegetation was ripe; mimosa and bougainvillea spilled from rotting trellises. At the top of the stairs, hidden away behind a peeling white wooden fence, was a small house with a disorderly garden in front of it. At the far end of the garden stood a short dark man at an easel painting a tall dark man, smoking a cigarette, carrying a sword and shield, and wearing an ancient Roman helmet and nothing else.

"*Ciao,* Tomás," Cara Boleri called.

Without taking his eyes off his subject, Tomás called back, "*Ciao,* Cara."

We entered the garden together, and Cara Boleri said something to them in Italian, presumably explaining who I was because the model turned to me and said, "I adore Americans."

"*Adora tutti,*" said Tomás, then, to me, in a stilted English, "How do you do?"

"Fine. *Buon giorno.*"

"*Basta,*" said the model, breaking his pose and walking over to me to shake my hand. "Paco Da Silva"—he smiled—"*enchanté.*"

My time at the nudist camp had accustomed me to the sight of naked people engaged in incongruous activities, but this was the first, and last, time I would see a naked Roman gladiator with a cigarette in his mouth.

"What do you speak?" Paco Da Silva asked me.

"Speak?"

"Languages. English gives me how do you say a sour throat."

"A little French."

"*Mais très bien, mon petit chou. Très bien.*" Then, to Cara Boleri, "*Il est mignon, ton petit américain.*"

We went inside and had a glass of Orvieto, sitting in the small, cluttered living room, full of Tomás's vivid paintings. He specialized in nude males and surreal still lives of vegetables. There were several large oils of scary-looking cucumbers.

In a corner, above a lacquered Chinese trunk, was a painting of Cara Boleri. She was lying on a couch, near an open window, afternoon light bathing her naked body.

I took the painting in, then turned away, only to see that she had seen me looking at it.

"What you think?" she asked me.

"*Bella.*"

"*Grazie,*" she replied, treating me to a very small smile.

We spoke several languages, occasionally switching back and forth in midsentence. Cara Boleri said very little. She sat there, curled up, her shoes off, her big toe rubbing absently against her calf, taking everything in. When I caught her eyes she held them for a moment, not turning away. It was a habit she had, at first disconcerting to me, of looking right back at you when you looked at her.

Tomás played the flamenco guitar. Paco, who used to work at the Lido in Paris, danced to the music with great passion. A few hours later we wound up at a trattoria on the Via Angelo Brunetti eating pasta and drinking more wine.

Cara Boleri and I held hands under the table. Paco flirted with the waiter, a strikingly handsome young man, which annoyed Tomás. He and Paco had a little flare-up, then kissed and made up.

Paco turned to me and said, "We are going to go fuck now, Tomás and me, *pour nous excuser.*"

And so the evening broke up. It was already late, after eleven. We all walked back together to the Via Margutta and said *arrivederci.*

Cara Boleri and I continued, walking hand in hand, through the terra-cotta city. We stopped in doorways to kiss—sloppy, Chianti-and Parmesan-scented kisses. I didn't want the night to end, but I didn't have a key to the Brazzianis' apartment. And she had to be up early with the little Belgians.

She told me she would take a cab home. I held on to her, not wanting to let go. I could have spent the whole night walking the streets of Rome and kissing her.

"*Buona notte,*" she whispered in my ear.

"Tomorrow night?"

"No. Not tomorrow night. The night afterward perhaps."

It was the *perhaps* that bothered me when, lying in bed later that night, I replayed the evening in my mind. I didn't understand. Her kisses had not been coy.

And why not the following night? What was on her schedule? Were the Belgians going out? If so, why didn't she say so?

Oh, I would find out why, eventually. It would be another lesson in my *éducation sentimentale*. But at that moment, full of the memory of wine and kisses, I was consumed with impatience. The prospect of waiting forty-eight hours to see her again seemed unbearable.

*   *   *

It wasn't until late the following afternoon that I saw Giovanni again. I was sitting at a café in the Piazza del Popolo very slowly sipping a caffè con latte and ignoring the annoyed look of the *cameriere,* who no doubt would have preferred that the table be occupied by people who consumed more than 200-lira cups of coffee, when I saw him drive by. On a Lambretta.

I squinted over my sunglasses, like Marcello Mastroianni in *La Dolce Vita,*[23] to make sure that the tall thin figure driving the motor scooter with a scarf around his neck was indeed my ex–fraternity brother.

I stared after him, wondering when he had found the time to learn to drive a motor scooter in the two days since the walk in the Villa Borghese.

I didn't have the opportunity to ask him that night because Giovanni had a meeting with one of his law professors and was not home for dinner. Nevertheless, I decided to take advantage of the Brazzianis' hospitality and have dinner with them.

We ate poached salmon with a very fine linguini, lubricated with a bottle of Valpolicella. Signor Brazziani told me about his year as a junior secretary in the Italian embassy in Washington. He went on at some length about his first experience with hominy grits, which,

[23]Vide supra, p. 64.

he claimed, was the most inedible dish he had ever been served in all his years in the diplomatic service, worse than anything he had ever had to eat in Eritrea, Borneo, or even Upper Volta.

That night I was up late with Camus when I heard Giovanni's key in the door. I glanced at my watch. 1:30. It seemed a very late hour to be returning from a meeting with one's law professor.

I fell asleep in a maze of confused thoughts and feelings and was awakened by one of the maids telling me I had a phone call. Out in the hallway, I picked up the phone and said, *"Pronto?"*

"Come stai?"

"Linguini," I replied, adding a qualifying *"Garibaldi."*

She laughed. I felt my knees go a little squishy. I would have done anything at that moment to see her laugh.

We made a date to meet at seven o'clock that evening at the café on the Via Margutta, beside the courtyard that led to Tomás and Paco's place.

We ciao-ed each other and hung up. I was standing there in my underwear, still in a daze, staring longingly at the phone, when Giovanni walked by.

"Good morning," he said.

He looked none the worse for wear from his late night at the professor's.

"Are you seeing Cara tonight?" he asked, loading his briefcase with law books from a shelf in the hall.

"Yes. We're doing some more sightseeing."

"Bravo." He smiled a little grimly and walked out of the apartment.

*   *   *

At seven sharp I was sitting in the corner of the little bar on the Via Margutta waiting for her. A song played over and over on the jukebox, a silly little song that was very big at the time in Rome. It was in a haphazard mixture of French, Italian, and Arabic, and, like everything else that spring, it made very little sense.

> *Cheri, je t'aime, cheri je t'adore*
> *come la salsa di pomodore*
> *Mustapha, ya Mustapha*
> *Mustapha, ya Mustapha . . .*
> *Tu m'as brulé avec une allumette*
> *Et moi je t'ai donné une de mes cigarettes, etc.*[24]

I would hear it all spring long. Everywhere. People would hum it in the street and on the bus. Paco loved the song and would belt it out in a gutsy falsetto until Tomás threatened to throw him out of the house.

A few minutes before, or was it after, eight she walked in. For a moment, she stood in the doorway and squinted her dreamy, unfocused Monica Vitti squint, searching for me. When her eyes landed on mine, I felt the tomato sauce rise in my veins.

We sat on a bench in the Villa Borghese and necked. If you could call it that. I'm surprised we weren't arrested for indecent behavior. If I'd had either a hotel room or a car, we would have gone there. But with no place to go we drove out to the Via Appia Antica on my Vespa. This time, however, we didn't stop at the villa with the rusty gate. She told me to continue beyond it, and we drove for miles, out to where the lights from houses were few and far between.

We finally stopped at a dirt road and got off the scooter. She took my hand and led me down the road. About a hundred yards in,

---

[24]Roughly: "Dear, I love you/Dear, I love you/Like tomato sauce/Mustapha, hey, Mustapha/Mustapha, hey, Mustapha/You burned me with your match/And I gave you one of my cigarettes."

there was a clearing, illuminated by the rising moon. We climbed over a low fence and walked out into the middle of the clearing. She took my jacket and laid it down on the dewy grass, then lay down on top of it.

"*Vieni, caro,*" she whispered, looking up at me. She continued to whisper things to me in Italian as I lay down beside her.

"*Adesso,*" she said, "*facciamo l'amore.*"

I started to move on top of her, but she stopped me. She got up and took her clothes off. I lay there on my back, watching her.

She stood over me, backlit by moonlight, and said in her breathy whisper, "You too."

I slipped my clothes off, and, as I lay there on my back, she straddled me, then very slowly lowered herself on top of me.

During bad moments of my life, when I am caught in traffic and listening to the cacophony of car horns blaring, or when I'm feeling a dentist's drill closing in on the nerve, I try to evoke those moonlit moments in that field off the Via Appia Antica. But they never come back beyond a series of little disconnected flashes. Not even by writing about them can I bring them fully back to life, except as a progression of words on paper.

As the years go by and as the memory gets fainter, the moment drifts farther and farther away, like a satellite leaving its orbit to wander endlessly in space. The signals get fainter and fainter until there is nothing but a barely audible beep.

When I dropped her at the gate of the villa that night, I told her that I loved her. She shook her head.

"Don't talk about *amore*. That's no good. Just be in love, okay?"

Wise words, and completely impossible to live up to. I know that now, but I didn't know it then. All I knew then was that there was nothing else in my world but her.

I held on to her, until she broke away and said she would see me again the day after tomorrow.

"Why not tomorrow night?"

"Because I have something I must do."

"What?"

"It is not important," she said as she opened the gate and walked inside. Just before she closed it, she blew me a kiss.

*   *   *

When Giovanni was absent for dinner again the next evening, I knew what the so-called unimportant thing was.

That night I stayed up and waited for him. It was nearly two o'clock when he entered the apartment. I was sitting in the study, an unread book in front of me, and as he passed the entrance, he saw me.

He met my eyes and knew why I was waiting for him. He took a brief look down the hallway toward his bedroom, then turned back, entered the study. Closing the door behind him, he walked over to his father's desk, stood there for a moment, then said, "*Finito*. It's over."

"What is over?"

"Our little ménage à trois."

He sat down beside me on the leather couch and looked at me with both compassion and annoyance.

"For a while it was amusing, wasn't it?"

"I'm sorry," I said. "If you had said something to me about her, if you had said she was your girlfriend . . ."

"It would have made no difference."

"But that first night, how come you told me you didn't know how to drive a motor scooter?"

"Because she wanted you to drive her home."

I looked at him, puzzled. "You see," he continued, "it had very little to do with you and me. We were both completely in her hands."

"I don't understand."

He shrugged. "There is nothing to understand. She is yours."

I let the words go through me, both thrilled and confused.

"Are you okay?" I asked, somewhat patronizingly.

He looked at me as if that were the stupidest question in the world. Which it was. How could he be okay? How could any man who was dumped by Cara Boleri be okay?

"Tell me something," he said. "That first night, in the Villa Borghese? Was she squeezing your hand?"

I nodded. He laughed.

"Why are you laughing?"

"Because she was squeezing mine as well."

I started to laugh too. We laughed for a while, but it was hollow on both our parts. In a simpler world we would have fought a duel, but there in that very civilized apartment in Rome near the Villa Borghese, we didn't fight. We laughed.

When we stopped laughing, he got up and said, "Now I must go to sleep. I am very tired."

After he left I sat for a long moment, afraid to move. Part of me, the part that was still the New York street kid with the scorecard, was basking in my victory. But there was another part of me, a part that was just beginning to take root, that felt a deepening and exquisite sadness.

I had finally begun to grow up. From that moment on I would never look at women the same way. I would understand why men killed themselves for love. I would cry at operas.

The next day I found a cheap pensione on the Via Sistina, not far from the Via Margutta. And that night I told the Brazzianis I was leaving and thanked them.

They were all three sitting at the dinner table as I stood in the doorway with my backpack. They urged me to sit and have dinner with them, but I was meeting Cara Boleri in an hour.

Signor Brazziani looked at me and nodded. I was convinced that he knew exactly what had happened. His rheumy eyes missed nothing. They probably had seen what I didn't see that first night at dinner—that I was to be Cara Boleri's next meal.

"*Arrivederci,*" he said.

"*Ciao,*" I replied, "*e grazie tante.*"

"*Buona fortuna,*" he added, and there was in those words of good luck the implication that I was going to need it.

* * *

For the next three months I lived a life that I would never live again. It was as intense and beautiful as it was lazy and aimless. I learned to be a master of the great Italian art of *far niente*—an art virtually unpracticed in the Anglo-Saxon world.

Cara Boleri left the Belgians and moved in with me in my little room on the Via Sistina. We made love at night, and in the morning she would go to church to confess the sins of the night before. We would walk in the park, take rides on the Vespa through the Trastevere or out to the beach at Ostia.

We had long lunches with Tomás and Paco. Now and then, Giovanni joined us, between classes at the law school. He had met another girl, a tall, blond, somewhat dense Lufthansa stewardess named Hedwig, who spoke little Italian or English, and so we added German to our little fruit salad of languages. Paco was convinced she was a lesbian.

"She look like she want to lick Cara's pussy," he whispered to me when she left the table for the *gabinetto.*

The days passed rapidly in this sybaritic fashion. Late spring merged into early summer, and the hot, funky smell of Rome began to rise from the cobblestones. After my money was gone, Cara Boleri got some from her parents in Biella, an industrial town north of Milan. But we went through that, and our *dolce vita* began to fray at the corners.

There was so little verbal communication between Cara Boleri and me that when the edges of our life got threadbare, there was no way to talk about it, not to mention a common language. I remember asking her why she had to go to confess our lovemaking to some priest in a dark confessional as if there were something wrong with it. She delivered an angry diatribe in a mixture of Italian, French, and English and then crossed herself.

And so we began, unconsciously perhaps, to look for a way out. My way out arrived in the form of a letter from my sister telling me that she was getting married in early July, three months sooner than she had planned. Her prospective husband, whom she had met while I was in Europe, wanted me to be his best man.

It was a port in the storm—not a particularly good one, but it would suffice. If it wasn't for my sister's wedding, I might not have had the strength to leave. I might have wound up working in a Fiat factory with ten *bambini* to feed.

* * *

Like a true coward, I didn't tell Cara Boleri I was leaving until two days before I had to get on a train to Paris, and then to Le Havre to catch a boat back to New York.

We were walking in the Villa Borghese. It was a hot Sunday, and the park was full of overdressed families strolling. Cara Boleri had been to mass that morning and had eaten the body and drunk the blood. She was wearing a very pretty but somewhat severe dress. To soften the look, I bought her a pink balloon. She let it trail in back of her as we walked, not saying very much, as usual.

Whether by accident or intention, we came upon the bench we had necked furiously on back in March. We sat down, and I turned to her and told her straight out what I had to tell her. After I was finished, she let go of the balloon. It floated up and away over the orange tile rooftops of Rome and disappeared into the smudgy blue sky.

Two days later, she stood on the platform of the Stazione Termini on a cloudy morning and waved good-bye to me. She was crying. So was I. It was like the farewell scene from an old movie, the smoke rising from beneath the train, the lovers gazing stoically through the steamy window at each other, the mortality of love floating up and over the station.

There were subtitles on the screen. On the soundtrack some bluesy Bud Powell played.

As the train pulled out, I watched her get smaller and smaller, until she was a speck of color dissolving in the mist.

I suffered all the way to Florence and most of the way to Le Havre. I was halfway across the ocean before I got a decent grip on myself. And when we steamed into New York, the fever broke, and I started convalescing. Never to be completely cured.

Somewhere out there in space, the lost satellite continues to beep. Very faintly.

V

THE MANN ACT

transportation of a minor across a state line for immoral purposes, which purposes include, but are not limited to, sexual intercourse, whether consensual or not.
                                           —Rep. James Robert Mann

Since its passage by the United States Congress in 1910, the Mann Act has struck terror into the hearts of men. The penalties involve long terms in federal prisons, whose inmates are not known to be particularly sympathetic to "child molesters." If you lived somewhere in the middle of Montana, you probably didn't have to worry much about the exact location of state borders, but anyone who grew up on the eastern seaboard knew exactly when he was crossing over the line.

On the one hand, there was a certain collateral benefit to the legislation in that it made us all better students of geography. On the other hand, it also made us very nervous about taking a trip with an underage girl across the George Washington Bridge to New Jersey or up the Hutchinson River Parkway to Connecticut.

I am not entirely sure when the statute of limitations kicks in for violations of the Mann Act, and I'm frankly too embarrassed to call my lawyer with a hypothetical question. "Seymour, listen, I was just curious about a friend of mine who, thirty years ago or so, took his seventeen-year-old baby-sitter up with the family for a weekend at his house in Lake Hopatcong, New Jersey, and they wound up shorthanded for a poker game . . ."

So let me state unequivocally, right here and now, that nothing that follows in this chapter is, strictly speaking, true. Nevertheless, just to be on the safe side—as Seymour would doubtless advise me if I wanted to spend the $450 a ten-minute phone conversation with him would run me—I will refer to this fourth Karen in my life as Karen ——; and the school where I worked when I met her, still in existence and having, I am sure, top-notch legal talent on retainer, will be referred to as the —— School.

As the sixties drifted toward the seventies and as things heated up in Southeast Asia, young males of my generation became increasingly preoccupied with ways to avoid being sent to Vietnam. Those who believed that it was a just and necessary war simply didn't want to get blown to bits; and those who, like me, believed that if we were going to take sides in a civil war on the other side of the world at least we could back the right side were even less eager to get flown back at government expense in a body bag.

I was within the draftable age window, eighteen to twenty-six, and not married. I was not the father of children, teaching school, or working in a defense-related industry, and so I had no reason to believe that I wouldn't be called up soon.

There was a great deal of folklore at the time about how to get out of the army by failing the physical. You could play either crazy or gay; but as more and more amateur crazy or gay acts were performed, fewer and fewer legitimately crazy or gay men got out. The army psychiatrists just got pissed off and started approving everybody.

So when I showed up for my physical at Whitehall Street Induction Center in Manhattan at 7:00 A.M. on a hot June morning in

1969, I put my hopes on a deviated septum. I didn't see how I could operate an M-1 rifle if I wasn't breathing correctly, and I was prepared to say so.

Along with a couple of hundred other young men, I wandered around the building, up and down elevators, in and out of rooms, in my underpants and socks, getting probed and prodded by a team of army doctors, undoubtedly from the lower percentiles of their medical school graduating classes.

I passed with flying colors, my deviated septum not even getting a notation on my paperwork.

I now had maybe a month or two at most to get a deferment before getting my head shaved. The prospect was sufficiently daunting to make me even more determined to find a way out. Riding the E train back to Queens, I hit upon an idea that could have landed me an exemption by remanding me to a mental institution instead of to the army.

My mother threatened to have me committed when I explained my scheme to her. It was simple and, as far as I could tell, foolproof.

It involved my getting married. To her.

I tried to lay it out for her very calmly and rationally, aware that on the surface it seemed a little bizarre. Bigamy, I explained to her, was a crime against an individual, actually against two individuals, and not ipso facto a crime against the state. Provided, of course, that the state didn't know about it. And why should it? And provided, as well, that neither of the two wronged parties brought an action against the bigamist. And, given who they would be, why should they?

She sat perfectly silent, her hands folded in front of her, not even blinking.

I went on.

Now if she and I were to find some justice of the peace in an obscure little town out in Jersey and produce a birth certificate with her maiden name on it, how would the justice of the peace know we were mother and son?

Her face darkened a shade.

"As soon as I submitted the marriage license to the draft board and got my deferment, we could destroy the license, see?"

Her face became a shade darker.

Then, to sell it, I added, "We can even have Dad be the witness."

"You are a very sick boy," she said and left the room.

So why am I telling you about my draft physical and my attempt to marry my mother in a chapter that is supposed to be devoted to my adventures with the Mann Act and yet another Karen? Because it explains what I was doing teaching English at a fashionable but poorly paying private school for young women on the Upper East Side of Manhattan.

After I'd passed my physical and been turned down in marriage by my mother, my last hope was a teaching job.

I went to the library and found a book with the names and addresses of all the private schools in the United States. I copied down as many names and addresses as I could until my hand hurt and the postage got extravagant. Then I wrote a form letter, made copies, and mailed them off to two hundred private schools.

To show how serendipitous our lives are, how timing dictates which roads we travel on our individual odysseys and with whom, I received a letter of interest from a prep school near Akron, Ohio, a few days before I received the letter of interest from the fashionable but poorly paying Upper East Side private school that my underage Karen attended and under whose auspices I violated the Mann Act.[25]

[25]Vide supra, disclaimer, p. 79.

In spite of the fact that at any moment I could get the dreaded summons to report to Fort Dix, New Jersey, to begin my basic training, I did not immediately contact the school near Akron. Even though Ohio compared favorably to the Mekong Delta, I didn't like the idea of living near any place where they manufactured tires.

So, foolishly, and, as it turned out, fatefully, I waited, gripped by inertia, like someone letting his money ride on a craps table and hoping that no one rolls a seven.

On the Friday before the first of August, the date I had set for calling the school in Ohio to accept the job, I received a letter from the headmistress of a school that, as explained earlier, must remain nameless.

Dear Mr. L——,

I am in receipt of your letter of July 30th. As it happens, we have recently had an unexpected opening in our English Department for which you may be suitable. Would you be good enough to phone me at your earliest convenience to arrange an interview? If you haven't as yet read Henry James's *Portrait of a Lady,* please do so at once.

Very Truly Yours,
Miss Constance A. Turnbill, Headmistress

I ran out and found the Cliffs Notes for the James novel, then phoned Miss Turnbill. Her voice on the phone was as peremptory as her letter.

"Three o'clock sharp, please. Give the doorman your name."

In spite of the season, I put on a corduroy sport jacket, my only one, a relatively narrow tie, and a pair of oxfords with argyle socks.

The doorman of the Stanford White building on Park Avenue looked at me askance, but he rang up to Miss Turnbill and obtained permission to admit me.

Miss Constance Turnbill came to the door and peered at me quizzically over her mother-of-pearl reading glasses, as if I were some sort of delivery she was not sure she'd ordered, then ushered me into a chintzy living room with lots of books and overpolished furniture. We sat in matching wing chairs on either side of a defunct fireplace.

"You, of course, know the reputation of the —— School," she began.

"Yes," I lied. All I knew about the —— School was what I had read in *The Handbook of Private Schools*—that it was all girls, extremely pricey, and located on the Upper East Side of Manhattan.

"We educate the daughters of some of the most prominent people in New York and have been doing so since 1911,"[26] she continued. "We are, therefore, very particular about our faculty. You majored in English at . . . ?" She lifted her reading glasses onto her nose in order to consult my query letter and mentioned the name of my sub–Ivy League college[27] in the tone of voice that one uses in discussing one's less successful relatives.

She peered back over her glasses, scrutinizing me again before saying, "You're terribly young."

I had just turned twenty-four, which to me wasn't all that young, but I saw no reason to contradict her.

"Perhaps, that might work in your favor," she went on. "Our seventeen-year-old girls have focus problems. If they focus on you,

[26]Not the real date of establishment of this school.
[27]Since I have only recently succeeded in eluding the attention of this school's rapacious alumni fund-raisers, I hesitate to draw attention to my association with it here by identifying it.

and if you focus on Henry James, we might actually accomplish something. You've read *Portrait?*"

"Several times."

"It is quintessential James, especially for young women. You shall teach it in the winter, but to start off, you'll do *The Scarlet Letter.* A little old-fashioned Puritanism will do them some good, don't you think?"

"Absolutely."

"You're not married, are you?"

It was clear from the way she asked the question that marriage was not something you wanted on your résumé in applying for a job teaching Henry James and Nathaniel Hawthorne to unfocused seventeen-year-old girls at the —— School.

I shook my head.

"Good," she said. "May I be candid with you?"

"Of course."

"There's a great deal of misdirected sexual energy within these young girls. They will direct it at you, and you will direct it at literature, and through a sort of indirect process of transference we may actually teach them something."

"Well," I said glibly, "James was a master of indirection," quoting a line from the Cliffs Notes.

That sealed it. I was offered an annual salary of $4,800 and told to report to the —— School for teachers' orientation the Friday before Labor Day.

So instead of dodging Viet Cong land mines, I became a focus of the sexual energy of a group of precocious seventeen-year-old girls. A job, as you will see, that was not without its own jeopardy.

I identified my Karen with little difficulty from among the Daphnes, the Phoebes, the Isadoras, the Anastasias in my senior

English class. Standing in front of the class the very first day, in my corduroy sport jacket, hands deep in my pockets, I spotted her immediately. She sat in the first row, directly in front of me, her blond hair so blond that it almost blinded you. Underneath the blondness and the very blue ingenuous eyes was an expression of intense febrile vacancy. She looked completely oblivious and completely absorbed at the same time.

Right away I realized that this wasn't going to be an easy job. These girls had grown up in Manhattan, the daughters of prominent writers, artists, journalists, psychiatrists, and were jaded beyond their years. They dressed expensively, if eclectically, radiated an aura of exquisitely honed ennui and were by and large neurotic. At the —— School, Fridays were half days in order that the entire school, students and teachers alike, could visit their psychiatrists.

They read widely and erratically, wrote with great flourish and very little respect for grammar. In addition to teaching Hawthorne and James, I was charged by Miss Turnbill with teaching them simple English punctuation so that they wouldn't embarrass the school later on at Bennington or Sarah Lawrence.

Like everyone else who went to high school in America at the time, I'd had to read *The Scarlet Letter.* I remembered it as an ordeal. The second time through was no easier. This time, however, I identified heavily with the Reverend Arthur Dimmesdale, as he stood in the pulpit mouthing piety in the face of his own misdirected sexual energy. I, too, stood in my pulpit, in this case the third-floor classroom looking out on East Eighty-ninth Street,[28] and mouthed symbolism, metaphor, and subtext in the face of the heated gaze of my Hester Prynne.

[28]Not the actual location.

Karen —— was the daughter of Jasper ——, one of the leading Jungian therapists in New York, and Katherine Breen ——, who had been a classmate of Mary McCarthy at Vassar and who wrote complex and intense novels about complex and intense women.

How two such intellectuals could have produced a daughter who had trouble getting through a set of Cliffs Notes is an anomaly of breeding.

During my English class, Karen —— never took her eyes off me. It was like driving directly toward a car with its high beams on. She sat in her seat, her legs crossed in front of her, looking up at me expectantly, anticipating every word out of my mouth.

She had a best friend, a tall, nearsighted, leggy girl named Iphigenia Gottleib, the daughter of Gustave Gottleib,[29] a professor of romance philology at Columbia. Iphigenia, or Iffy, as the girls called her, lived downtown near the ——s' apartment on lower Fifth Avenue, and after school I would often find the two of them riding the same bus downtown that I was on.

They would wave to me from their seat in the back and get off at the same stop I did. At the time I was apartment sitting for a wealthy aunt and uncle in their spacious, nicely furnished apartment at Fifth Avenue and Tenth Street while they traveled around the Mediterranean on a yacht.

The doorman was an alcoholic Frenchman named Maurice. He operated the elevator, and one of his favorite little jests was replying to my "*Ça va, Maurice?*" with "*Ça monte, et ça descend.*" It was Maurice who told me that the two girls were hanging around the building trying to find out if I was in or not.

"I am completely discreet, monsieur," he assured me.

I wasn't sure if by being discreet he meant that he was not furnish-

---

[29]Author of the book *Speaking Provençal in Fourteen Days.*

ing the young girls any information about my whereabouts, or if he meant that if I chose to entertain young girls in my aunt and uncle's apartment, while they were away in Europe, he would turn a blind eye.

*   *   *

Uptown at the —— School, meanwhile, I thought it was time to see how my students wrote and assigned a short essay on Hawthorne's use of symbols in the first hundred pages of *The Scarlet Letter.* This topic is covered in the Cliffs Notes and, predictably, I received a few artfully plagiarized variations on the Cliffs' Ph.D.-for-hire's analysis. But not from Karen ——. This is what I got from Karen ——.

Hawthorne uses symbolism to talk about repressed sexual feelings in Puritan society in America in the eighteenth century. Especially the hypocritic minister Reverend Dimmesdale who tries as hard as he can to deny his feelings for Hester but can't so he gives all sorts of boring sermons in church and says nothing while Hester has to wear the A on her breasts in spite of herself. I think it's an example of sexual hypocracy [sic] and that Dimmesdale should have to wear an A on his pants which is where he has repressed feelings. Beside being boring this book has too many pages of description and too many symbols. They should just do it and tell everyone else to deal with their own problem. In conclusion Hawthorne uses symbols to hide his own sexual hypocracy [sic].

Putting aside for the moment the spelling and sentence structure and the fact that she had the wrong century, the essay was at least original and to the point. Let's face it: Nathaniel Hawthorne has been responsible for generation after generation of high school students having to plow through turgid, overwritten fiction that has nothing to do with their own lives.

A teacher-student conference seemed in order, and so I asked Karen —— to come see me after school to discuss her essay. I was sharing a small office with a history teacher named Herbert Kalmbach.[30] He was an imperious, balding man with a bad postnasal drip. His desk and mine were up against each other, and Karen —— and I discussed Hawthorne's Puritanism against a steady counterpoint of shifting phlegm, as he corrected his students' exams.

It was mid-September, the weather still warm, and she was wearing a light cotton dress that couldn't have passed the —— School dress code by very much. The dress code was essentially whatever Miss T, as she was referred to by the girls, thought appropriate at any given moment. Girls were sent home in the middle of the day if, in the opinion of the headmistress, their attire reflected poorly on the —— School.

Frankly, I was surprised that Karen —— had made it past Miss T that day. The dress material was exceedingly thin, and though you couldn't actually see anything underneath it, you thought you could, which is a lot more distracting.

We got off to a shaky start.

"Well," I said, tautologically, "your essay reflects a certain amount of reflection on the subject."

"Does that mean it's good?"

"Good is . . . well, it's the effective expression of thought that is clearly rendered in an expressive manner," I said, slipping into redundancy again. "The thing is . . . your essay does make a point, which is good. There's not a lot of ambiguity in it, though things could possibly have been better said . . ."

"Like what?"

"Well, for instance, there's this sentence, 'Dimmesdale should have to wear an A on his pants which is where he has repressed feelings . . .'"

"What's wrong with that?"

---

[30]No relation to the Watergate personality of the same name.

"For one thing, the relative pronoun *which* is not set off in a sub-ordinate clause, which leaves ambiguous the exact location of his repressed feelings. I mean, obviously it's not the pants that were re-pressed but Dimmesdale himself. Do you see?"

"Oh."

"Precision in language is important."

"But *you* understood what I was saying, didn't you?"

I ignored the question and went on. "And, of course, you have Hawthorne in the eighteenth century instead of the nineteenth."

"I thought he wrote the book in 1850. Didn't he?"

Kalmbach got a kick out of this one. He actually chuckled out loud.

"Yes, but, you see, 1850 is in the *nineteenth* century."

"How come?"

The meeting lurched forward until Kalmbach, apparently unable to contain himself any longer, left the office, closing the door be-hind him. It got very warm. I suggested that we wrap things up. She suggested that we ride the bus downtown together.

At 4:30 on a hot September day it's a long ride down Fifth Av-enue from Eighty-ninth Street to Tenth Street. We sat side by side, all the way downtown, my thigh in its Robert Hall wash 'n' wear slacks occasionally making contact with her wafer-thin-cotton-covered thigh. She offered me a Tootsie Pop, which I declined. She told me about her parents. Her opinion of them was not much higher than her opinion of Arthur Dimmesdale.

"Daddy's crazier than half his patients." She went on, indiscreetly dropping names of his famous patients and describing their ail-ments to me.[31]

We got off together at Tenth Street. She lived at number 1, a large

[31]It is not generally known among literary scholars that John Dos Passos suffered from dyspareunia.

modern building on the west side of the street, near the park, favored by doctors and wealthy divorcées enjoying extravagant alimony settlements.

"Can I see your place?" she asked.

"It's actually not my apartment. It belongs to my aunt and uncle. They're in Europe."

"Just for a couple of minutes?"

To his credit, Maurice didn't raise an eyebrow as we got into the old elevator and creaked up to the fourth floor. The stale odor of Burgundy floated through the car. Karen continued to suck on her Tootsie Pop, which, though I was a good number of years younger than Humbert Humbert, didn't make things look any better. As he opened the elevator door to let us out, he winked at me.

My aunt Carol and uncle Kermit had been theater producers in the forties, and the apartment was colorfully furnished. There were framed Playbills in the hallway, photos of them with Odets, Kazan, Lee J. Cobb et al. They had bought Kandinsky, Braque, Man Ray when they were still affordable, and there were examples of their work throughout the apartment.

"This is so great," Karen —— exclaimed as I took her for a tour, pointing out the artwork and telling her a few anecdotes that Carol and Kermit had told me over the years.

"You have anything to drink?" she asked, when we got to the kitchen.

"Glass of water?"

"Uh-uh." She shook her head.

Though we hadn't crossed a state line, the drinking age was eighteen at the time in New York, and I did not want to contribute to the delinquency of a minor—at least not by giving her alcohol.

"How old are you?" I asked.

"What difference does it make?"

"A lot."

"I just turned eighteen."

"Then how come you're just beginning your senior year?"

It was the wrong question. I knew it before the words were completely out of my mouth.

"Why do you think?"

She broke into tears. Sniffling loudly, she reached into her Bloomingdale's pocketbook and took out her wallet and a driver's license with her date of birth on it: September 7, 1951. She had turned eighteen a week ago.

I poured her a small glass of Carol and Kermit's amontillado. She sat down at the kitchen table, and the sniffling died away. Sipping her sherry, she told me that she had been left back in the sixth grade, but that it wasn't her fault because Jasper and Katherine had dragged her through Europe that year and she never learned fractions right.

The failing Indian summer light came in from the window and made her flimsy cotton dress seem even more insubstantial than it was. I knew I had to get her out of there. Eighteen or not, she was my student, not to mention a very confused young girl.

"I'm afraid you have to go," I said, after she had finished what was left of the sherry. "I've got a dinner appointment."

"With who?"

"With whom," I corrected.

"You are *such* a teacher."

I walked her to the elevator, which took forever to come. I shuffled from foot to foot. She played with her hair. When the door opened, Maurice looked at me as if he were disappointed. *"Déjà?"* his Gallic eyes seemed to be asking.

* * *

Karen —— was not in English the next day. I felt her absence in the same way I felt her presence. There was a force field in the room whether she was there or not. After class Iphigenia Gottleib came up to me and said, "Karen's got a migraine."

"I'm sorry to hear that."

"Maybe you should call her with the homework," she suggested. "She could do some extra work over the weekend. Catch up."

"Why don't *you* give her *your* notes?"

"I didn't take any," she replied shamelessly. Then: "Got to run. Can't be late for Dr. Toretzky." And she was gone, her knee-length plaid skirt whisking through the doorway to my classroom.

It was Friday, one o'clock, and everyone was heading for a psychiatric appointment, except the janitors and Miss T, whose mental health, as least as far as she was concerned, was exemplary.

I rode the bus downtown, thinking about Karen ——. And thinking about my thoughts about Karen ——. They were not good thoughts. She was taking up altogether too much space in my mind. She was just a screwed up young girl with a crush on her English teacher. I vowed to stop thinking about her.

With this in mind, I called Erika, my girlfriend at the time. Erika Phelps-Goodstein was a graduate student in comparative lit at NYU. She was writing her thesis on Thomas Mann's hypochondria and, in the process, she started to develop all sorts of physical ailments of her own.

When I suggested dinner and a movie, she told me she was suffering from a very bad stiff neck and had to sit in a chair with a heating pad on it.

"Would you like me to come over—we could watch TV?"

"I can't move my neck," she said crankily.

"I'm sure you'll feel better tomorrow."

"If I'm not in intensive care . . ."

So I was alone. At least until nine o'clock. I was sprawled out on Carol and Kermit's living room couch, watching a ball game, when the intercom buzzed.

"You have a visitor, monsieur," Maurice informed me. "A young woman."

Was it my imagination, or did he put emphasis on the word *young?*

As I opened the door, I saw Maurice standing in the open elevator, watching us, or, more accurately, watching Karen ———.

She was wearing a pair of jeans, a light sweater, the top two buttons undone, and heels. She had put a red ribbon in her hair and some bright red lipstick on her lips.

It was not an outfit you wore to discuss American literature with your high school English teacher.

"Hi," she said. "Iffy told me you could give me a makeup lesson for today. I had a really bad migraine. But it's better now."

I looked pointedly at my watch.

"I know it's a little late," she said, "but you don't go to bed at nine o'clock, do you?"

I let her in, if only to close the door on Maurice's steady gaze.

"May I have a drink please?"

"To discuss Nathaniel Hawthorne?"

"We don't have to talk about him, do we?"

I gave her a glass of sherry, and we sat at the kitchen table, and I listened to her talk about how she didn't want to go to college but instead wanted to move to New Orleans and be a bartender in the Spanish Quarter.

"Don't you mean the French Quarter?"

"There too."

She asked to use the bathroom, and I pointed her in the direction of the hallway to the master bedroom, where the bathroom was located.

After a few minutes, she called my name.

I found her in the bedroom sprawled on Carol and Kermit's brocade bedspread. Though she was fully dressed, her body language was clearly the pouting, sex-kitten language of a girl-next-door centerfold in *Playboy*.

I stood in the doorway and asked one of the dumber questions of my life: "What do you want?"

"I don't know."

I folded my arms and tried to look stern. "Listen. This isn't a very good idea."

"Why not?"

"I think you know why not."

"Don't tell me you're a—"

"No, I'm not. But that's beside the point. You're my student and I'm your teacher. And you're a lot younger than me."

"Not a lot," she said, accurately.

"Look, you're a very pretty girl, and—"

"Oh, forget it!" And she sprang up and walked right past me out of the bedroom. She stalked down the hallway, her heels clacking loudly on the parquet floor, and out the door.

* * *

During the next week I got the ice treatment at school. Not only from her but from Iphigenia Gottleib and, it seemed to me, from the rest of the class as well. We were wrapping up *The Scarlet Letter*, and neither they nor I would miss it. But just when I thought I was finished with Hawthorne for good, I was summoned to Miss

T's office to be told that he wasn't quite out of my life yet.

"We have the senior class's fall trip coming up," she informed me. "We go to Boston and, since the girls have just finished reading *The Scarlet Letter,* we'll make a side trip to Salem. To see the Custom House."

"Very appropriate."

"Quite. And it would seem appropriate, as well, that you be one of the faculty members accompanying the class, seeing as you have just finished teaching Mr. Hawthorne."

I started to utter some impromptu excuse, but it was soon evident that it wasn't a request but a direct order.

"We're taking the train a week from Monday. Nine A.M. sharp. We'll be staying at the Ritz Carlton."

So in the middle of October, at the height of the foliage season, I found myself on the train for Boston, along with Constance Turnbill and forty-five senior girls from the —— School. Arthur Dimmesdale returning to the scene of the crime.

I sat beside the headmistress in the rear of the car, so that we could observe the girls in front of us. In accordance with Miss T's directive, they were all dressed in a manner befitting the image of the school, largely in young women's Ann Taylor suits, flats, and Burberrys. I was dressed in a manner befitting my $4,800 annual salary.

Miss T sat with a volume of Swinburne's verses, her posture discouraging conversation. I read a copy of *The New Yorker,* my eye periodically drifting over the top of the page to see Karen —— sitting beside Iphigenia Gottleib, the two of them wearing matching Burberrys, in a seat facing the rear of the train. Every time I chose to look in their direction, Karen ——'s eyes met mine.

It was past four o'clock when we checked into the Ritz Carlton. Fifteen minutes later, lest we waste a precious moment of our time

in Boston, we were marching around the Common, then up Newbury Street and over to Beacon Hill. It had all been scheduled with
military precision. By sundown we were back at the hotel, for another fifteen-minute respite before dinner.

We ate at an Italian restaurant in the North End, at two long tables with a preselected menu of overdone veal parmigiana and
spaghetti. The headmistress and I each presided over a table. The
presence of Miss T kept giggling and loud talking at a minimum. I
spent dinner chatting with Anastasia Greeley[32] and Daphne Snow[33]
about their summer in Europe. As they described their trip to
Rome, I imagined a pink balloon floating over all the places they
had visited.

We returned to the hotel in cabs. The girls' rooms were on two
different floors, with the headmistress and I each having a room on
one of them. In the lobby Miss T informed me that it was my duty
to do bed checks at 10:30 P.M. on my floor.

I asked her what a bed check involved.

"You knock on the door," she explained, "and when it is opened,
you verify that the requisite number of girls is present and accounted for," intrepidly agreeing subject and verb.

"Do you think that's an appropriate job for me?"

"Why wouldn't it be?"

"Well, since they may be in their nightclothes, wouldn't they be
more comfortable with a woman doing the bed check?"

"Frankly, I'm not concerned with their comfort, or yours. I have
no intention of doing two floors' worth of bed checks. And since

---

[32]Her real name. Anastasia Greeley went on to a distinguished career as a hyperreal-
ist artist, best known for her exquisitely rendered paintings of Harley-Davidson mo-
torcycle engines. In 1979 she married a real estate developer named Horace Greeley
and changed her name to Anastasia Rabinsky.

[33]C. P. Snow's illegitimate grandniece.

drummed out of the ——— School, shipped off to Vietnam to have my guts ripped opened by a mortar shell.

I was prepared to have all that happen as I looked at her in all her glory standing a few feet away from me. She smiled at me a little smugly, as if to say, "You're not going to turn *this* down, are you?"

How could I? What a cruel blow to a young girl's ego to have a man walk away from her after she's thrown her raincoat out the window for him.

So it happened. It was very nice, if I remember correctly. But, to tell the truth, not quite as earth-shattering as I thought it would be during all the times I had imagined it. I suspect she felt similarly because afterward she gave me a sisterly kiss on my forehead, got up, appropriated my Ritz Carlton bathrobe, and went back to her room.

I slept badly that night and was barely awake on the bus to Salem at nine the next morning. She sat two rows in front of me, chatting with Iphigenia Gottleib, wearing a cardigan sweater on top of her sensible suit.

As we walked around Salem, visiting the Pioneer Village and the Nautical Museum, she seemed lighter, more carefree than I had ever seen her before. And along with this insouciance was a little smug grin. She chatted pleasantly with me over our box lunches, relaxed and uncharacteristically articulate. And that night she was in her room for the bed check.

In my room I lay in bed and waited for hours for the knock on the door. It never came. I was relieved it didn't. And I was deeply disappointed.

* * *

When I got back to the ——— School, I asked the registrar for Karen ———'s school records. There were a number of reports of disciplinary problems, poor schoolwork, dress code violations. I looked at her test scores and realized that she was not dumb; she was just lazy.

But what really got my interest was her date of birth: June 17, 1952. She wouldn't be eighteen till the following June. The driver's license was phony. There it was in black and white. I had violated the Mann Act. I was a fugitive from justice.[34]

She came to see me one more time at my apartment. It was a cold day in December, and she showed up wearing a new Burberry. I offered her a glass of sherry, and we sat in the kitchen in silence for a few moments.

Finally, she said, "I guess I should apologize, shouldn't I?"

I shrugged dismissively.

"You could have gotten into a lot of trouble."

"More than I thought," I said.

She looked at me blankly, and I told her about checking her school records for her correct date of birth.

"Oops," she said.

"It's okay. Unless, of course, you're going to tell me you're pregnant."

"I can't have children. I have an incompetent cervix."

"Sorry."

"It's all right. I'd be a lousy mother."

She finished her sherry, and we sat in silence for a moment before she said, "Can I see you when I'm eighteen?"

"Sure," I replied, knowing it would never happen.

"We'll just have to survive till June."

She leaned across the table and kissed me good-bye. But it wasn't a sisterly kiss. It was on the mouth, her tongue halfway down my throat.

It was typical of Karen —— that she couldn't leave well enough

[34]Vide supra, disclaimer, p. 79.

alone. The kiss was her way of rubbing it in. See what you're going to be missing. Eat your heart out.

We both survived very well till June. Though we occasionally rode the bus together downtown, she never showed up on my doorstep again. I gave her a very charitable B— in English.

June came around, and she was graduating—going to BU, everybody's fallback college, thanks, in large part, to a very nice recommendation from her English teacher.

At the graduation ceremony, she introduced me to Jasper and Katherine and told them I was the best teacher she had ever had. Nobody, she said, had ever explained *The Scarlet Letter* better than I had.

I watched her get into a cab with her parents, on their way to Tavern on the Green, and drive out of my life forever.

* * *

The day after graduation, as I was cleaning out my desk for the summer, Miss T appeared in the doorway and asked if I would mind coming down to her office for a little talk. We walked downstairs to her well-appointed office, with the Chippendale desk and the Currier and Ives prints on the wall. I sat across from her on the hard, padless chair, a chair that was not designed to be sat on with any sense of comfort.

"Well, it appears as if you've risen to the challenge," she said.

"Thank you."

"Our senior girls are safely on their way, many of them to excellent colleges."

I nodded, throwing a little half smile of modesty in her direction.

"I was, however, quite surprised to see the results from one or two of our less gifted students. Karen ——, for instance."

She looked at me carefully, but I didn't flinch.

"I would have thought a B− in English beyond her talents," she said.

"She worked very hard."

Once again I met her eyes. We sat like that for a good ten seconds, neither of us looking away.

Finally, she said, "Be that as it may, we are going to be bringing young men into the —— School come September, an accommodation, I'm afraid, to time and change."

"An inexorability."

"And it would seem to me, therefore, that our young ladies will have a new focus for their attention."

"I would hope so."

"Therefore, I must tell you quite honestly that I think the stratagem you and I discussed last August is now contraindicated. They might actually do better with someone else teaching them senior English, perhaps someone a bit older than you."

"Of course."

Then, as if to clear up any doubt I might have had about whether or not I had just been fired, she got up, offered me her hand, and said, "Thank you. Your final check will be mailed to you."

As I rode downtown on the bus, a small carton filled with personal items in my lap, I thought about the line from *Death of a Salesman*.

What happened in Boston, Willy?

Did Miss T know?

I would never find out. Which was just as well. There are some things in life you never need to know, and whether or not Miss T knew what happened in Boston is one of them.

*   *   *

Since then whenever I am back in Boston, I make it a point to stay at the Ritz Carlton. On the ninth floor, if possible, with a window giving on Newbury Street. A glass of sherry in my hand, amontillado if they have it, I look out the window and imagine a Burberry floating slowly to the ground like a leaf in the wind. Then I get into bed with a copy of *The Scarlet Letter* and read myself to sleep.

VI

HEART OF DARKNESS

The Selective Service stipulated very clearly that it was the obligation of the registrant who had received a teaching deferment to notify his draft board immediately in the event that he was no longer engaged in education. Though the penalties were stiff, I decided to wing it for a month or two in order to buy time to find another way of avoiding being shipped off to Vietnam.

I didn't dare broach the subject of marriage again with my mother. And the thought of requerying the two hundred private schools I had queried only a year ago did not appeal to me. I was through teaching *The Scarlet Letter.*

So I was both depressed and a little panicky, not to mention broke, when I walked into a post office one day to pick up mail that had been forwarded from my last address, an apartment I shared on East Sixth Street with a sculptress[35] who had turned her bathtub into a repository for wet clay as a way, I'm convinced, of getting rid of me. By 1970 there were no longer any army or navy recruiting posters on the walls of post offices in the East Village. This war wasn't going over well with my neighbors, and every time someone hung a "Join the Army and See the World" poster on the wall, it was either defaced or removed. But there was a recruiting poster for the

---

[35]A non-Karen named, if I remember correctly, Lenore Kimbrough, who married a drummer from Pink Floyd and used an NEA grant to make a series of silkscreens of his scrotum.

Peace Corps, which showed smiling young men and women having adventures in far-off places. Someone had written on it in Magic Marker—WHAT A TRIP!

I knew from the extensive folklore of draft avoidance techniques prevalent in my neighborhood that service in the Peace Corps was a deferment from military service. The problem was that you needed to have a particular skill to teach people in underdeveloped countries. The skills I possessed at the time were not necessarily useful to others.

In the spirit of leaving no stone unturned, however, I got an application from the clerk and filled it out on the spot. In the section marked "Language Skills" I put French and Italian, an exaggeration, perhaps, but not one completely without basis. After all, I had exchanged passionate endearments with Cara Boleri in a patois of French and Italian.

As it turned out, it was thanks to my so-called language skills that I was accepted into the Peace Corps, sent to teach English to French-speaking students at the Lycée Sylvanus Olympio, in Lomé, Togo, and wound up meeting Karen Ogbomosho, the only Karen in my life who was named after a city.[36]

She was also the only woman in my life whom, strictly speaking, I have ever offered money for sex. There were, however, mitigating circumstances, as you will see, which led to this act of desperation.

After a cursory FBI background check, which did not turn up my summer at the Sunnydell Ranch, my naked emergency landing at the Allentown airport, or my alleged violation of the Mann Act,[37] I was sent to Howard University in Washington, D.C., for training.

[36]A city in southwestern Nigeria, present population 514,900. For purposes of cultural comparison, imagine a woman named Karen Albuquerque.
[37]Vide supra, disclaimer, p. 79.

Togo, we were informed, was six degrees north of the equator and very hot. It was the home of an eclectic variety of tropical diseases, from dengue fever to schistosomiasis, an illness brought on by a microscopic worm entering your body through the soles of your feet while you are bathing in shallow streams, then incubating deep inside you for six years, before turning your urine black, your skin yellow, and slowly and painfully killing you. To this day I carry in my wallet a United States Peace Corps–issue disease card that lists all the exotic tropical diseases I was exposed to in Togo. In the event that I collapse someday in Grand Central Station the doctors will know what to look for.

They speak forty-four different languages in Togo, a country about the size of West Virginia, and French, brought by the colonialists, serves as the lingua franca. In Washington we were forbidden to speak English with one another and were reduced to communicating in French and in a number of obscure African languages spoken by very small and isolated populations. Fewer people speak Ewe,[38] the principal language of Togo, than live in Staten Island.

After a month of Peace Corps training, which consisted of French, structural linguistics, African history, tropical hygiene, mountaineering (rapelling down bleachers in the Howard University field house), and irrigation, I was shipped off to Lomé, the capital of Togo, a country without any sizable mountains and with an annual rainfall of 652 inches, for two years' service teaching English.

Unlike most Peace Corps volunteers, hard-core idealists just out of college, I had no desire to get sent off to the bush. My colleagues headed off intrepidly into the hinterland with their kerosene

[38]356,957, per 2000 census.

lanterns, malaria tablets, and camp beds. I chose to stay in the capital, closer to some of the comforts of home.

Though hardly a booming metropolis, Lomé had amenities such as electricity and running water, not to mention bars, restaurants, and discotheques. It was at that time a picturesque little city that possessed one of the finest beaches in West Africa.

The British built roads, schools, and hospitals in their colonies. The French brought Molière, boeuf bourguignon, and fellatio to theirs. Though nearby Ghana and Nigeria were much more developed, Togo was the place you wanted to be. I was provided with an apartment on the coast road, about fifty yards from the beach. It was a breezy place, with large windows giving on the ocean, creaky old colonial furniture, and intermittent electricity.

The Lycée Sylvanus Olympio[39] was a couple of miles away, ten minutes in my Peace Corps Jeep, a green topless Willys with diplomatic license plates. My duties there were not demanding—two courses in the morning, one in the afternoon, after a siesta. The students wore khaki shirts and shorts and were exceedingly polite. *"Oui, monsieur, non, monsieur, pardon, monsieur."*

They were endearing, these young Togolese struggling with the arcane features of the English language. We bypassed *The Scarlet Letter* and went straight to *i* before *e* except after *c*.

But to be perfectly honest, I hadn't come to Togo to develop my skills as a teacher of English. I was, frankly, more interested in the exotic charms that West African life had to offer a young man in the early 1970s. And, with this in mind, it didn't take me long to discover the nightlife in Lomé. Much to the dismay of William.

---

[39]Sometimes referred to as the George Washington of Togo, Olympio was assassinated in a coup reportedly engineered by his brother-in-law, Nicolas Grunitzky, whose Polish father, a phosphates engineer, was said to have had seven Togolese wives.

William came with the apartment. Or so he told me. I discovered him on the stairway the day I moved in. He was a tall, gaunt, ageless man, anywhere between thirty and fifty. He was, he informed me, the houseboy, and, as such, it was his job in life to serve the occupant of the apartment, whoever he might be. I asked him how much he was to be paid for this service.

"Nothing, master," he replied. He pronounced the word ma*stah*, stressing the second syllable. He had learned his English at a missionary school in Ghana and spoke it colorfully, if erratically.

Now in addition to doing our jobs teaching English, digging septic tanks, or building irrigation ditches, Peace Corps volunteers were supposed to be promulgating American culture and values. Slavery not being among them, I told William that I wouldn't be able to accept his kind offer because it was in violation of the Thirteenth Amendment to the United States Constitution. He looked very unhappy and slouched off down the stairs.

But he didn't go away. Like Melville's Bartleby, he remained on my stairway, night and day, until I eventually agreed to hire him. The most I could induce him to accept was 1,000 CFA[40] francs a month, a little less than four dollars. Since the Peace Corps gave us seventy-five dollars a month spending money, over and above providing a place to live and a Jeep, it was well within my budget.

William slept in a hammock on the back porch and cooked me variations of chicken, rice, fish, and *foo foo,* the staple diet of Togo. *Foo foo* consists of peeled yams, boiled and pounded in a large wooden mortar with an oar, then garnished with a fish, meat, or peanut sauce. It has the consistency of saltwater taffy and is eaten from a communal bowl with your hands.

---

[40]*Communauté Financière Africaine,* the official currency of Togo, whose exchange rate at the time was roughly 250 CFA francs to 1 U.S. dollar and about ten times that on the black market.

William insisted on waiting on me from the kitchen. He gave me a little bell that I was supposed to ring, but I just called his name when I was ready for the next course, and he shuffled in in his straw sandals to clear away.

If I had one failure as a Peace Corps volunteer, it was that I was never able to teach William how to mix a drinkable martini. He had a very heavy hand with the vermouth bottle.

In addition to his inability to conquer the martini, a not insignificant shortcoming in a houseboy, William was overly concerned with the state of my soul. The missionaries had gotten to him big time when he was a schoolboy in Ghana, and he was the only African I ever met who was a prude. He disapproved of my lifestyle and let me know about it.

"Mastah, you bring shame on house. The Lord does not embrace you in His bosom. You are in the shadow of the valley." And so forth.

*   *   *

My fall from grace was largely due to the discovery, about a month or so after my arrival in Lomé, of Même Mère, Même Père. To call it a bar, a disco, or even a whorehouse wouldn't really do it justice, though it combined elements of all three. Its name derived from the fact that Togo was a polygamous society, and people would often introduce their siblings by saying that so-and-so was a brother or sister and adding the qualifier *même mère, même père* (same mother, same father).

It was located on a side street, not far from the only movie house in town, Le Fleur de Lys, essentially a sheet hanging on the wall and about a hundred rickety seats that specialized in old French movies featuring Fernandel and Louis de Funès, which you could barely see through the haze of Gauloises smoke.

You entered Même Mère by walking through a bead curtain into a large, dark room with a bar, a dance floor, tables, and a garish mixture of red, green, and blue tinted lights. You could barely see anything inside, or hear anything, for that matter, because the music was always just a notch below the threshold of pain.

The music was nonstop high life, a deceptively simple West African dance that vaguely resembles the salsa. Like skiing, it requires coordinated hip motion and a good sense of rhythm. Neither of which I possessed.

The first time I walked into the place, early on a weekday night, it was not very crowded. There were a few girls dancing by themselves and a couple more at the bar. I sat down at a table in the corner, which featured a candle in a painted glass struggling to stay lit, and ordered a beer from a girl in bright African dress with large ivory earrings.

The girls, all of them in colorful dresses with scarves on their heads, wore sandals or were barefoot. And as far as I could tell in the very dim light, some of them were very pretty. I began to have what William referred to as "ungodly thoughts."

Back in Washington we had been given a fairly nauseating description of the various venereal diseases we would be exposed to should we interact too intimately with the people of the host country. In spite of this caveat, the United States government didn't see fit to issue us condoms along with the antimalaria pills and copies of *The Autobiography of Benjamin Franklin* that were given us in large quantities.

I'd had the foresight, however, to stock up abundantly before leaving Washington. In the words of my roommate at Howard, Timothy Gillen, a cesspool engineer from Shaker Heights, Ohio, who was digging ditches up in Dapango near the border of what was then Upper Volta, I was betting on the come.

It didn't take long to be approached by a man in a dashiki and sunglasses. He stuck out his hand, and said, "Peace Corps?"

"Yes," I replied, shaking his hand.

"Gbedey, Jean François, at your service."

"Vous parlez anglais?"

"Better than king of England." And he broke out into a broad laugh. I joined in. We laughed for a while, then he asked, "You like girl?"

What I thought he said was, "You like *girls?*" because I nodded.

He snapped his fingers, and within seconds another girl came over carrying two beers. She uncapped the beers, poured each of us a glass. As she did this, he said something to her in Ewe and she went back to the bar.

"You like this girl?"

"Yes," I answered, in an effort to be polite. We drank some more beer, while the girl who had served us started dancing with one of the other girls. The two girls gradually moved in front of our table and began to dance for us.

"You like *this* girl?" he asked, indicating the other one.

I got the point.

During our Peace Corps training our instructors had empha-sized that the philosophy of the organization was to adapt, as much as possible, to local mores. Our job was not to import American customs to the host country but, rather, to lend our technical and scientific expertise to help solve their problems.

With this in mind, I had the following thoughts, more or less si-multaneously. I was thinking about how the Peace Corps philoso-phy of one-on-one, person-to-person interaction applied to this situation. I was thinking about the catalog of horrific venereal dis-eases we had learned about in Washington and their incubation pe-riods. I was thinking about the whole notion of paying for sex and what it meant in terms of my ego and the reputation of the Peace Corps in particular and America in general. I was thinking about whether I had enough CFA francs on me to cover whatever the price might be and what impact that might have on my seventy-five-dollar-a-month budget.

Mostly I was thinking about the girl on the left. She was dark-skinned, with tribal markings on her cheeks, just below her eyes. When she danced, she barely seemed to move her hips. She had beautiful white teeth.

Gbedey, Jean-François, invited both girls to sit down at our table. More beers arrived. Nobody took any money from me. The girls spoke French, and we limped through a conversation of sorts.

"*Vous aimez le Togo?*" the one on the left, whose name was Kumla, asked me.

"*Beaucoup.*"

"*C'est bien.*"

"*Oui, c'est bien.*"

We drank more beer. I was given a high-life lesson by Kumla. She told me I danced very well. I admired her tactfulness. After the sixth beer, I began to lose focus. I told Gbedey, Jean François, that I thought I'd better go home while I could still drive the Jeep. When I asked him what I owed for the beers, he waved me away.

"Nothing?"

"Next time."

What he said next really threw me. "You take both girls with you, okay?"

I blinked. Several times.

"They like you," he added.

Even though neither girl apparently spoke English, I took him aside and said, "I appreciate your hospitality, but I'm not sure I can afford this."

He looked at me with an injured expression on his face. "Afford?" he said. "Do you think I have an ill-repute house here?"

I shook my head quickly. He removed his sunglasses and looked me directly in the eye. "You will never pay money for girls in my house. *Jamais.*"

"Thank you," I replied. We shook hands, like diplomats who had just negotiated a treaty. Then he put his arm around my shoulder and walked me outside. Both girls were already in the Jeep, Kumla in front, Kasi in the rear. I got in the Jeep, waved to Gbedey, Jean François, started the engine, let out the clutch, and bounced off down the unpaved street toward my house.

William's face darkened considerably when I walked up the stairs with the two girls. Judging by the tone of voice he used in addressing them in Ewe, he must have thought that they had picked me up on the street and forced me to take them home. They snapped something right back at him, and we walked past him to the bedroom, closing the door behind us.

"*La salle de bain, c'est où?*" Kasi asked me. I pointed to a doorway off the bedroom. They took me by the hand and escorted me into my own bathroom, which had a toilet, a bidet, a sink, and an old chipped-tile shower with about seven minutes of lukewarm water if no one had used any within the past hour.

They looked around, appreciating the relative opulence of my bathroom, and then started to remove my clothes. I tried to explain that with all the beer I had drunk I needed to pee. When my French failed me, I used sign language. They said something in Ewe, then led me over to the toilet and very matter-of-factly unzipped my fly to assist me.

This was a local custom that had not been covered in our course in African sociology in Washington. When I was finished, Kumla took me into the shower, and we were soon joined by Kasi. The three of us played under the tepid stream until the water got cold, and then, sharing a towel, we dried off and piled into bed.

We rolled around the bed, happy with beer and fresh from the shower. We climbed all over one another, cavorting like puppies. As Karen Myers would have said, it was very polymorphous. I wish I could remember more of the specifics (you probably do too).

Eventually, we collapsed and lay there, dead to the world under the mosquito net, until we were woken in the morning by the disapproving voice of William informing me that I would be late for school.

I showered while William made me a cup of very strong coffee. As I sat drinking it, he stood in the doorway of the kitchen and read to me from Paul's First Letter to the Thessalonians (chapter 4, verse 3):

For this is the will of God, even your
sanctification; that ye should abstain
from fornication.

* * *

And so I became a regular customer of Même Mère. Some nights I would take someone home with me; other nights I would go home alone. There was only so much polymorphous sex I could deal with on a regular basis. Kumla and I became pals. I would buy her beer, and she would tell me, in her schoolgirl French, about life in the village in the north where she had been born. Sometimes, she would even recommend other girls for me to take home.

Though a lot of beer flowed under the bridge, money never changed hands. Just as he claimed, Gbedey, Jean François, was not running a whorehouse so much as a bar where girls liked to drink beer, dance, and go home with *yovos*, the Ewe term for white people.

Though Même Mère may not have been, strictly speaking, a bordello, it apparently wasn't the type of place that Peace Corps volunteers were encouraged to frequent. And it didn't take long for it to be brought to the attention of my superiors that my Jeep was parked in front of the bar several nights a week.

I was called in to have a talk with the head of the Peace Corps mission in Togo, a retired professor of theology at Purdue. Bud Little[41] was a big, florid, athletic man in his early sixties, who had been with us in Washington and liked to have heart-to-heart conversations, which he referred to as bull sessions.

We sat in his office, furnished with an assortment of Benin bronzes and other African objets d'art that he had accumulated since our arrival in Togo.

"Let's have a little bull session, you and I, my friend," he said. He took out a pipe, lit it, leaned back in his chair, and said, "It seems that you are mixing with the Togolese quite extensively . . ."

"That's the idea, isn't it?"

He nodded, puffing out his cheeks in a painful smile.

"Perhaps, but there are appropriate and nonappropriate accommodations to local customs. Just because you are in Rome, you don't do everything that the Romans do, do you? For instance, you wouldn't go to the Colosseum and watch people be devoured by lions, would you?"

I shook my head emphatically.

"So, let me put the butter right on the bread for you, all right?"

Bud Little was partial to folksy aphorisms. We were always being

---

[41]Director of the Peace Corps in Togo (1970–71), who was sent home on medical leave due to a particularly stubborn case of gonorrhea that proved resistant to antibiotics. Little maintained that the infection was contracted from a bathtub that, unbeknownst to him, had been used by his houseboy.

admonished not to put the cart before the horse or tell tales out of school. Or, my favorite, to churn butter back into cream.

"You have apparently been frequenting a brothel. Now the Peace Corps is not in the business of being your parents—"

"What brothel?" I interrupted.

"I believe you know the place I'm talking about. It's on the rue des Martyrs, near the movie house."

"Même Mère?"

"Yes."

"That's not a brothel."

His eyebrows narrowed. "That's not what I hear. Several people have reported seeing you leaving the place with a girl in your Jeep."

"Well, that's true . . ."

"Do you know these girls?"

"Sort of. I mean, I meet them and we drink beer and we dance the high life and we talk . . ."

"And you take them home and have sex with them, don't you?"

"Well, yes, but I don't pay them any money."

He looked at me long and hard.

"You don't pay them *anything*?"

"No."

"Absolutely nothing?"

"Well, I buy them an occasional beer, but a beer costs about a dime here."

"Let me understand this. You go there, you meet a girl, you buy her a beer, then you go home and have sex. And you don't pay them anything?"

"I don't always go home with someone. Sometimes I go home alone."

"I don't get it."

"Bud, have you ever been to a singles bar in Manhattan?"

It was his turn to shake his head.

"It works the same way," I explained. "Except there you don't get away for a dime. It's Bloody Marys at two dollars a pop."

"Well, I'll be damned," he murmured. He shook his head a few more times, then started to launch into the hygiene conversation, but I cut him off.

"Don't worry," I assured him. "I brought a gross of Ramses with me."

"A gross?"

"Uh-huh. Probably a little optimistic, but as Barry Goldwater[42] says, 'Extremism in the defense of liberty is no vice,' right?"

I must have been churning butter back into cream because he just sat there shaking his head and muttering, "Well, I'll be damned."

* * *

And so I spent my time teaching compound tenses at the Lycée Sylvanus Olympio by day and hanging at Même Mère by night, with occasional frolics under the mosquito net. Then one evening I was sitting at my table at Même Mère discussing the difference between the angle of a white woman's and a black woman's buttocks with Gbedey, Jean François, when I saw an attractive woman at the end of the bar, drinking a glass of wine and examining what appeared to be a large book. In all the time I had spent at Même Mère I had never seen anybody drink anything but beer or whiskey, and I had never seen anybody read anything.

[42]Former senator from Arizona and unsuccessful presidential nominee in 1964, Goldwater, in a speech no doubt written for him by Pat Buchanan, said this.

"Who's she?" I asked. "I've never seen her in here before."

"She's not from here."

"What's she doing?"

"Giving me trouble."

I squinted at her for a better look. She was tall, well-built, with beautiful skin and some very nice-looking jewelry.

"Is that a book she's reading?"

He exhaled slowly and said, "She is looking at my money, you understand?"

I shook my head.

"She is my partner."

"No kidding."

"She make my ass hurt," he said, with the air of a man who had suffered long at the hands of this woman. She got off the barstool, came over to our table, and engaged in an animated conversation with Gbedey, Jean François, in Ewe. Neither seemed to like the other one very much. When they were finished, she turned to me and said, "Ogbomosho, Karen, please to meet you."

Even here in Togo, six degrees north of the equator and on a completely different continent, there were Karens in my path.

"How do you do?" I said.

Close up, she was even more striking. Unlike most African women, she looked you straight in the eyes, directly, almost con-frontationally.

"I hope you are not allowing Mister Gbedey to fill you with too much untruth. He is a man of much ignorance."

At this point, Gbedey, Jean François, said something sharply to her and got up, and walked over to the bar.

"Would you like a drink?" I offered.

"Perhaps some other time," she replied and went back to the bar, where she and her partner had another animated exchange.

* * *

A few evenings later she let me buy her a glass of wine. I learned that she was born in Nigeria, in the town whose name she bore, that she had been educated in Lagos, and that Gbedey, Jean François, was her cousin. She had loaned him the money to buy Même Mère several years ago and had not as yet seen any return on her investment. And she wasn't very happy about it.

"Look how he runs this place," she said. "Everybody steals from him. These girls drink beer, don't pay him anything."

"Yes," I pointed out, "but they bring in customers."

She gave me a condescending look, as if to say, What do *you* know? What *did* I know? I was a schoolteacher, not an expert in the West African bar business. I was also a customer. She seemed to be aware of this fact because she said, "You, for example. You take home girls from here, do you not?"

"Well . . ."

"Why else would you come here?"

It would have been very difficult to claim that I was there for the decor or the quality of the beer.

"But I am not a . . . *client*." The French word sounded more delicate.

"Why not? You don't like girls?"

"I like girls."

"So why are you not a customer?"

"What I meant is, and I don't make a habit of it, and when I do . . . take home a girl, I don't pay her anything."

"*That* is the problem," she said. "Why should you not pay anything? You should pay something to the girl. And the girl should pay something to us. We provide the store."

"The store?"

"Yes, of course. We are the store. The girls are the merchandise. You are the customer. That is how you make business."

You didn't need an M.B.A. from Wharton to see her point. Même Mère was not an efficient business. And I, as a member of the United States Peace Corps, whose mission it was to bring Togo into the modern world, was not helping matters.

Not knowing what else to say, I asked her to dance.

"No, thank you," she said.

Dancing did not interest Karen Ogbomosho, nor, apparently, did drinking or dining. It took several invitations before she agreed to have dinner with me. There was a place called Chez Roger, which was run not by Roger but by a Togolese named Kodjo Kpakpa,[43] who claimed to have studied cuisine at the Cordon Bleu in Paris. I had eaten there a few times and was convinced that Kodjo Kpakpa had never been anywhere near the Cordon Bleu or, in all probability, Paris. His idea of coq au vin was boiling a chicken to death in a pot filled with Algerian Burgundy.

She declined my invitation to pick her up, arriving instead in a very clean Renault Ondine, which looked immaculate parked beside my dust-laden Jeep. She was wearing a gorgeous dress made of a rich-looking fabric. It was the type of dress you saw on African diplomats' wives and cost a lot of money.

I learned very little about Karen Ogbomosho during that dinner, or afterward. She was vague about the details of her life, her family, what she did everyday, besides run herd over her cousin. She was smart, even witty, but she didn't seem to take any pleasure from repartee. There was something terribly literal about her. To me, though, her lack of coquetry merely made her move alluring.

She had high cheekbones and very smooth skin. Her eyes were deep brown, set off by a tint of eye shadow. Her body, or at least what I could see of it under the fabric of her dress, was lovely.

---

[43]The onomatopoetic Ewe name for duck.

I very much wanted to become acquainted with that body, but it didn't look as if I was going to be permitted anywhere near it. There was nothing at all about her that would give a man any hope. And yet I continued to spend time with her. That night, and other nights when she would agree to have dinner with me or to walk along the beach, I kissed her, and though she didn't turn away, her lips were not responsive.

I tried to get her to come back to my place, but she always refused. Nor did she invite me to her house, wherever that was. One night I tried to follow her home, but the Ondine easily lost the Jeep on the coast road.

Every time I asked Gbedey, Jean François, about her, his eyes looked skyward and he would say something like "She is on earth to make my life miserable." And that was about the extent of it.

The girls at Même Mère didn't like her either. Kumla called her an *emmerdeuse* and blamed her for the fact that I had stopped inviting her, or any of the other girls, home.

I became fixated on Karen Ogbomosho.

William, of course, was thrilled at finding me alone in bed in the morning.

"You have seen the lights, mastah."

"No, William, I'm just striking out."

And yet I persisted. I don't know why. Maybe I would have backed off if she weren't so unattainable, if her name weren't Karen . . .

My exasperation grew until one night, as I was sitting with her late in the bar of the Hôtel du Golfe, a run-down, colonial-era place frequented largely by nostalgic French expatriates, I put it to her straight.

"What's it going to take?"

I'd had a couple of Beck's and was feeling reckless. Swiveling on my barstool, I looked her in the eyes and said, "If I have to pay, I'll

when you think about it, I've already been paying for

th, considering all the food and drink I've been buying

o you mean?"

"I want to go to bed with you. And I'm willing to pay for the privilege, if that's what it's going to take."

"You want to pay me to have sex with you?"

"Only if there's no other way."

"Do you think I am a prostitute?"

"No. But you're a businesswoman, and I'm making you a business proposition."

"Lovemaking is not business."

"*Au contraire.* Didn't you yourself say that your cousin shouldn't let the girls go home with men for nothing?"

She was clearly caught in a contradiction. For a moment she thought about what I'd said. Then she finished her Singapore Sling, turned back to me, and said, "How much?"

"I don't know. You're selling, I'm buying. So it's up to you to set the price."

"In business," she said, "price is determined by what the buyer is willing to pay, is it not?"

"Okay. In that case, I'm willing to pay everything I have."

"Everything?"

"You can have the shirt off my back if you want."

She reached out to examine the material of my shirt, rubbing my collar between her thumb and forefinger. I thought she was joking, but Karen Ogbomosho didn't joke about anything, and especially not about money. She was actually evaluating my shirt, a colorful short-sleeve Hawaiian number that I'd bought in a secondhand clothes store on St. Mark's Place in New York for two dollars.

African women know a lot about fabrics. They run the markets, which do a lively trade in the imported textiles from which African clothes are made. So she must have realized the value of my shirt. And this is why I knew she had a soft spot for me.

"Okay," she said.

"You want my shirt?"

"Yes."

"That's all?"

"And you must pay for a room in the hotel, of course."

"Here?"

"Yes."

"Now?"

"Why not? How much money do you have with you?"

Reaching into my pocket, I took out whatever was there, a few thousand CFA francs, less than twenty dollars. She helped herself to most of it, got off the stool, and left the bar to see about the room. Five minutes later she was back.

"Room 24. You will wait fifteen minutes and then knock on the door."

Then she left me to wait a very long fifteen minutes. I went outside to get some fresh air. The hotel was pale stucco, with overgrown vines and thatched grottoes. Though it was nearly eleven o'clock, people were still eating. You could hear scattered, desultory conversations in French as the ex-colonialists lingered over their imported Camembert.

From the rear patio there was a view of the beach, sparkling in a full moon. I could hear the surf clobbering the shore, the same surf I heard every night from my second-story apartment about a mile down the beach.

I gazed blankly out into the ocean, marveling at the lengths to which men will go to fulfill their fantasies, feeling strangely detached. When it was time to go upstairs to Room 24, I walked slowly, like a man going to his execution. Sex by appointment is not unlike capital punishment. They are both acts of passion committed in cold blood.

I knocked softly on the door, waited, then pushed the door open and entered.

The room was lit by moonlight streaming in through the wide-open window giving on the ocean. She lay naked on the big four-poster bed, on her side, her head supported by one hand. The other hand rested on her hip.

Ingres couldn't have painted her any better. The diffused light, the composition, the dancing rays of moonlight on the ebony skin. You could have put a frame around her and hung her in the Louvre.

I felt light-headed, transfixed by the conflation of feelings and images—the beautiful woman, the painting, the funky breeze coming in from the Bight of Benin outside.

I stood there staring at her for so long that she said, "Well?"

"You're beautiful," I mumbled.

"Are you going to stand there looking at me all night?"

"If I want to. After all, I'm the customer, right?"

Even at this moment, as she lay there naked and vulnerable in the moonlight, about to give herself to me, there seemed to be no joy in her. I wondered how deep inside her the woman that she was was entombed.

I slipped out of my clothes, lay down beside her, and inhaled the musty aroma of Africa—coconut, jasmine, pepper, and licorice. Or perhaps it was casaba, yams, pearls, and chicory. Or maybe mango, palm wine, eucalyptus, and coffee. My left hand caressed her breast, my finger playing idly with her nipple.

There was a small sense of triumph as I felt her nipple harden beneath my touch.

She gave ground slowly, grudgingly, fighting herself every inch of the way. She was determined to keep things professional. And she wasn't doing very well. As my hand slipped down over her belly and downward, I could feel her businesslike demeanor dissolve into a puddle.

I had a sudden memory of Karen Myers saying that erections betrayed men. Well, there in Room 24 in the Hôtel du Golfe, Karen Ogbomosho had finally betrayed herself.

It wasn't long before my attempts at technique completely disintegrated. By the time I was inside her all the way, I was transformed into a Comanche warrior. I grabbed her hair as if I was going to scalp her. I screamed. She screamed back. With enormous strength, she pulled around on top of me and then we rolled over, clawing each other, twisting the sheets all around until we wound up in a tangled mess on the floor.

I was surprised we didn't have the hotel management up there with fire extinguishers. It was that out of control. And I knew, as soon as it was over, that it would be the last time she and I would ever make love. We had nearly killed each other. God knows what would have happened the next time.

We lay on the floor recovering, our breathing gradually quieting. This was not the time to make small talk. I got up quietly, dressed, and left as she lay on her stomach, clutching the sheets, her eyes closed.

Just before I left the room, I looked back at her as she lay on the floor, sweat glistening on her skin. I tried to absorb that picture so that I would remember it. I wanted never to forget it.

I walked home along the beach and went straight to bed, sleeping as deeply as a soldier after a fierce battle. The next morning William chose Second Corinthians for the breakfast Bible recitation. I told him to can it. I was in no mood.

* * *

I was not surprised when, the following evening, Gbedey, Jean François, informed me that his cousin had gone back to Nigeria. When I asked for her address, he looked at me strangely.

"You are not going there, are you?"

"No. I want to send her something."

I had William make up a package. He had skills in this area. I took the package down to the post office on the Place de l'Indépendance. When the clerk asked me, for the Nigerian customs form, what the contents were, I told him it was a shirt. When he asked me what the value was, I said it was priceless.

VII
ANNA KARENINA

*Why not put out the candle if there is nothing more to look
at?*

—Leo Tolstoy, *Anna Karenina*

*A*nna *Karenina was not her name.* It was Karen Mendoza. She
was half Puerto Rican, half something else, and she lived in a
strange dark apartment on West Ninety-sixth Street in Manhattan
with two cats and a dog named after poets.

We met on a rainy night in the mid-seventies when I picked her
up in my cab.

Taxi driving is not a deferment from military service. But by the
time I got home from Togo, the draft had become a lottery, and I
had number 327. The only way they were going to take me was if
the Russians sailed into Sheepshead Bay. And then, in '75, the last
helicopter took off from the roof of the American embassy in
Saigon, and I was out of the woods.

Driving a cab was the perfect profession for a fledgling writer
who was, in the words of his parents, still trying to find himself.
The majority of the people I grew up with were already living serious, adult lives, earning money, paying down their mortgages, fill-
ing their parents' wallets with photos of grandchildren. My parents
had very little in their wallets to show for all the time, energy, and
money they had spent raising me.

I had just turned thirty and was living in an eighty-dollar-a-month apartment over a Chinese restaurant, haphazardly trying to find myself. During the day I dabbled in literary pursuits—stories, poems, a dark Dostoyevskian novel entitled *Notes from the Rearview Mirror.* At night I drove a cab. Unlike musicians', my day job was my night job.

Several times a week, I would pick up a cab from the Rainbow Garage on Twenty-first Street, between Sixth and Seventh. It was one of the things I liked about being a cabdriver—you really didn't have to make a commitment to the profession. In those days, there were a lot of freelancers driving cabs. Any day you needed fifty to seventy-five bucks, you could call up a taxi garage at three in the afternoon to find out if they had a cab available, and they almost always had one available, especially if you were willing to drive nights.

I loved the serendipity of traveling all over the city in a completely haphazard manner. I loved trawling the avenues in a Ford Fairlane with bad springs and two hundred thousand miles on the odometer. I loved coming back into Manhattan late at night, after a run to the airport, over the upper roadway of the Fifty-ninth Street Bridge, my radio tuned to Symphony Sid,[44] listening to Mingus and watching the lights of the city blinking in the distance.

A taxicab can be a laboratory for the study of human behavior, a required course for an apprentice writer. If you pay attention, you can witness firsthand the exquisite banality of unguarded human communication; you can hear the entire gamut of lies and exaggerations, of hyperbole and bullshit.

It presents, moreover, a constant opportunity for improvisational

---

[44] Sidney Torin (1909–1984), popular jazz DJ on WJZ in New York, whose theme song ("Jumping with my boy Sid in the city/Mr. President of the DJ committee," et cetera) was based on a tune by the "late, great" Lester Young.

theater. You can pretend to be working as a taxi driver for any number of reasons. At times I told people in my cab that I was a Latvian immigrant, an orthodontics student trying to pay his tuition, a mob wheelman in the Witness Protection Program, the ne'er-do-well son of a cement magnate from Syracuse.

But with Karen Mendoza, I was just a cabdriver with a soft heart. I picked her up on the corner of Seventy-ninth and Columbus in the rain. It was coming down hard. She was standing with no umbrella and a dog with a red bandanna around his neck. She was wearing dark glasses. At eleven o'clock at night.

You generally avoid picking up people like this, but it had been a slow night. She gave me an address on West Ninety-sixth Street in an off-key, slurry voice. I figured she'd had a couple and decided not to engage her in conversation. You learn early on to avoid stimulating drunks in any way, because if they get too excited you wind up having to hose down the backseat of your cab.

We rode in silence up Central Park West, turned into Ninety-sixth and when we got to her building on the south side of the street, she gave me a five for a two-eighty-five fare and got out without waiting for her change. I figured it was a tip and watched her walk unsteadily toward a three-story brownstone, then quickly hooked a U and headed for Broadway.

In retrospect, I wonder how I knew that the small black notebook on the floor of the cab was hers. I found it when I pulled into the garage a little after midnight and checked the backseat, as I did every night, for objects left behind by passengers. We were supposed to report these to the dispatcher for the lost and found, but nobody bothered because it would involve paperwork. If you found anything, it was usually money, and to a cabdriver his cab is strictly eminent domain when it comes to found cash.

There was no name or address anywhere in the book, but there was no doubt in my mind that it belonged to the strange woman with the dark glasses and the dog with the bandanna. I can't tell you how I knew. I just knew.

I opened the notebook and saw that it was filled with poetry—page after page written in an erratic, hurried hand. The poems had titles such as "My Blood Runs into the River, Downstream," "Death Hallucination Number 34," "Where Have You Gone and Why?" As if the titles weren't enough, the last was dedicated to Sylvia Plath.[45]

Believe me, I didn't need to have anything to do with a woman who wrote poems to Sylvia Plath. A woman who went out in the rain at night in dark glasses without an umbrella, whose dog looked like he was painted by Magritte, could only be trouble. But instead of turning the book in to the lost and found or even tossing it, I took it home that night and read it.

Though they were weird, dark, even scary, the poems had a kind of gallows humor to them. If you can imagine poems about death and suicide being funny. They seemed to be written stream of consciousness, first draft, no revisions, like Mozart's score for the D Minor Requiem Mass.

I had a strange feeling about these poems—I felt as if they were a time bomb, as if I had to get them out of my possession before they blew up the tenuous construction of my life.

So the first thing I did when I picked up a cab at four o'clock the next afternoon was to drive up to West Ninety-sixth Street and check the names next to the buttons beside the door of her brownstone looking for a clue. Just exactly what I was looking for I couldn't tell you. Perhaps I thought I would find Edna St. Vincent Millay's name beside a door buzzer.

---

[45]American poet (1932–1963), married to the English poet Ted Hughes, who put her head in the oven in London in 1963, which may have precipitated the trend of female poet suicides that followed.

There was the usual goulash of ethnic names. In true New York fashion I pressed them sequentially, and in true New York fashion nobody responded. I went back to my cab, sat for ten minutes staring at the doorway, then remembered that I was on the clock and said to myself, in true New York fashion, "What're you—out of your fucking mind?" I could see Manny the dispatcher's face when I told him that I booked nothing all night because I was trying to return a notebook of lost poems to its owner.

I restarted the motor and was pulling back out into Ninety-sixth Street when I saw the dog with the red bandanna walking along the street, casually peeing on trees, alone. He was not only unleashed but unaccompanied. I slammed the brakes on, and double-parked. The dog sprinkled the trees along the street, then turned in to the building, went down the stairs to the doorway, and lay down in front of the basement door.

It was a quarter to five. I had already wasted forty-five minutes of my shift, having deadheaded uptown and sat in the cab in front of the brownstone watching the door. Manny was constantly threatening not to give us cabs if we didn't book enough money. There was one guy in the garage, Ira, who was so intimidated by the dispatcher that he didn't even stop to pee. Instead he carried a thermos under the driver's seat.

I decided to leave the notebook beside the dog so that she would see it when she let him in. I got out of the cab and walked over and down the three steps to the entrance to the brownstone. The dog gave me a little halfhearted growl. But it was strictly pro forma. This dog was a surreal dog.

Just as I was kneeling to leave the book, the door opened. I looked up and saw her in the doorway, lit in the setting early-winter sun. She was wearing a nightgown under a robe, socks, no slippers.

I stood back up, proffering the book. And that's when I saw her eyes without the dark glasses.

"Who is it?" she asked, looking beyond me, with that hollow, unfocused expression of the blind.

"The cabdriver that took you home last night."

"You brought my poems back," she said, almost matter-of-factly.

"Yes. You left them in my cab last night."

I handed her the book. She opened it, felt the pages.

"Did you read them?"

"Yes. They're very beautiful."

We stood for a long moment without speaking. Finally, I said, "I better be going. I have to go to work." I pointed back at the cab double-parked in front of the building before I realized that she couldn't see what I was pointing at.

"You can't just read my poems and go."

"I'm double-parked."

"Just leave them a note to ring my bell. It's the ground floor, rear apartment, 1B, Mendoza."

And with that she and the dog went inside. I checked my watch. Five o'clock. I'd have to keep the cab out late to make my nut. I could just walk away. I had accomplished my mission. I had returned the poems. But instead I wrote out notes for the two cars I had blocked in and put them on their windshields.

The apartment was lit only by shaded lamps. There was incense burning, Piaf playing softly on a stereo, a couple of cats. I sat down on the couch and was carefully scrutinized by the cats.

A few minutes later she emerged from the bedroom wearing a sweatshirt and jeans, her hair tied up in back, and crossed to the small kitchenette to make tea.

She negotiated the space around her with apparent ease. She

seemed to find exactly what she needed exactly where it was. Her hair was dark black, her skin light, her mouth full, as if to compensate for her eyes.

"What are your cats' names?" I asked, making conversation.

"Ted Hughes."[46]

"What about the other one?"

"Ted Hughes. They're both named Ted Hughes."

"What about the dog?"

"García Lorca."[47] She rolled the *r*'s beautifully.

Then she turned in the direction of the dog and called, "García Lorca, *ven aquí*." The dog didn't go to her.

"He never does what you ask him to do. I found him by the river. He only speaks Spanish. Someday he'll get run over by a truck. That's his fate. That's why I call him García Lorca."

"Was García Lorca run over by a truck?"

"No. He was killed by the Fascists. They took him out in the street and shot him. In the heart. Just like that. Early in the morning. In the rain."

I could see her body tighten. One of the poems in her notebook was called "Blood in the Gutter." It described the assassination of the Spanish poet by right-wing goons in such low-key language that it was chilling.

We drank the tea side by side on an overstuffed sofa, ignored by Ted Hughes and García Lorca. Conversation was sporadic. She would indulge in lengthy, expressive paragraphs that went off on tangents, then suddenly stop and sit silently for long moments.

---

[46]English poet, married to Sylvia Plath and, according to suicidal feminist poet folklore, the reason that Sylvia put her head in the oven.

[47]Federico García Lorca (1898–1936), Spanish poet, author of *Blood Wedding* and *The Poet in New York*, among other works, was killed by Franco's goons at the outset of the Spanish Civil War.

Her face and hands seemed always to be moving, reflecting light from their surfaces. From certain angles, she was exquisitely beautiful. From other angles she looked tormented.

As I sat talking to her, I became acutely conscious of her blindness. It was difficult adjusting to it. I found myself nodding or shaking my head, and, then getting no response, waiting for her to say something.

I wondered what she'd been doing out alone in the rain at eleven o'clock at night. I wondered whether García Lorca was a Seeing Eye dog. I wondered if she called both cats Ted Hughes, or one of them Ted and the other one Hughes.

It was after six when the doorbell rang and a pissed-off neighbor asked me to move my cab. I got up, thanked her for the tea, said good-bye.

"I'll see you again," she said, without a drop of irony. The way she said it, it wasn't a question or a statement so much as an inevitability.

"You never told me your first name," I said.

"Karen."

Of course.

At 9:30 I stopped at the Belmore Cafeteria, a cabdriver hangout on Park Avenue South, for something to eat. The food was ample and cheap, the conversation was shop talk. It was there that I learned about the methods of short-circuiting the hot seat[48] and about the existence of the 110th Street checkpoint.[49]

---

[48]In order to keep cabbies from taking fares off the meter, taxi companies experimented briefly with installing a weight-sensitive rear seat that would start the meter automatically as soon as someone sat on it. The system could be deactivated in about fifteen seconds by anybody with half a brain and a screwdriver.

[49]A early method of racial profiling: a cabdriver driving north of 110th Street on either Madison Avenue on the East Side or Eighth Avenue on the West Side with a fare of the wrong color could flick his headlights at 110th Street and would be followed to his destination by an NYPD patrol car.

That night, the night I met Karen Mendoza, I picked at a tuna sandwich and considered taking the cab in early and telling Manny I was sick. It was a risky thing to do. Manny could stop giving you cabs as punishment. As far as Manny was concerned, you didn't get sick.

But I drove my shift, keeping the cab out till after two in order to show up with a decent number on the meter. The number, however, didn't thrill Manny, who looked at my meter and said, "What'd you do—go to the movies?"

* * *

I didn't take a cab out the next day. Instead, I worked desultorily at my novel in progress. Unable to concentrate, I checked Information for her phone number. There was no listing for a Karen Mendoza anywhere in Manhattan.

At six I walked crosstown and took the Eighth Avenue subway up to Ninety-sixth Street. I rang the doorbell. It took a while for her voice to come across the intercom. "Who's there?" I realized that I had never told her my name. So I told her it was the cabdriver.

"Who?"

"The one who found your poems."

She came to the door wearing a bulky sweater and a long skirt, looking very different than she had the previous night. She even smiled at me—a strange, disjointed smile that completely disarmed me.

We drank wine, and I told her about my book. The more I spoke about my book, the worse it sounded. It was a book I would never finish. I have the manuscript somewhere in the garage with my back tax returns. Though unfinished, it presents a hard-hitting, lurid description of the existential bleakness of a young cabdriver living in New York over a Chinese restaurant in the mid-seventies.[50]

---

[50]Film rights available through International Creative Management, Beverly Hills, California.

After an hour of disjointed conversation, she asked me to take a walk with her. She held my arm as we walked west toward the river. García Lorca accompanied us. He sniffed and peed promiscuously, moving on ahead as if he wanted nothing to do with us.

We sat on a bench watching the dark clouds drifting over the river. She asked me to describe the way the river looked. It was like translating the world into another language for the benefit of a foreigner.

She slipped her hand into my jacket pocket. I can still feel it, small and warm against my side. For long periods of time, we said nothing. When we talked it was in little bursts, mostly monologues. I don't know how long we sat out there, but eventually the damp chill drove us home. García Lorca was nowhere in sight.

"Where is he?" I asked.

"Somewhere."

"Aren't you worried about him?"

"No. He'll come home when he's ready to come home. If he doesn't get run over by a bus."

Back at her apartment, she poured us more wine, then went into the bathroom. I heard the bathwater running. She came back out, wineglass in hand, and said, "I've run a bath for you."

Taking a bath in someone else's apartment was a very intimate thing to do. But then so was describing how the clouds over the river looked.

"It'll warm you up." She smiled. Again, it was the disarming smile, the smile that seemed to have nothing to do with her poems.

I went into the bathroom, took off my clothes, and got into the tub. The bathroom was candlelit, delicate and feminine. I luxuriated in the warmth, letting the hot water soak away the chill. I sipped my wine, closed my eyes, and drifted.

I floated over the Hudson with the clouds, moving west over New Jersey in a hot-air balloon, looking for the dog. Down on the ground, Franco's goons were hunting poets. Fog was rising in wet wispy puffs. I was a spy for the Abraham Lincoln Brigade, mapping the Royalists' positions . . .

My eyes were still closed when I felt a washcloth against my forehead.

"Keep your eyes closed," she whispered. "I want you to see how I see."

I kept my eyes shut as she washed me gently, tenderly, not so much cleaning me as exploring me. This, I realized, was how she looked at people. With her hands. She examined every inch of me, slowly but resolutely.

I heard her take her clothes off, then slip into the bathtub with me. Wrapping her legs around me, she pulled close, and I felt her warm against my chest. She rested her chin on my shoulder and put her arms around me.

We stayed like that, inhaling each other, until the water cooled. She rose, pulling me up with her, and wrapped us in one large towel. I kept my eyes closed as we patted each other dry, then she took me by the hand and led me into her bedroom. The blind leading the lame.

There was the scent of perfumed candles and chamomile tea. I heard Ted Hughes scampering around as we lay down on the bed. My eyes still closed, I explored her as she had explored me. Slowly, unsystematically, almost haphazardly, reading her with my fingertips like a blind man reading Braille.

When she put her hands on the back of my neck to pull me to her, I opened my eyes for a moment and saw her demented, beautiful look, her mouth twisted to compensate for her dead eyes. We kissed tenderly, then fiercely. And then she reached for me and took me inside her, uttering something fierce and guttural in Spanish.

It is always at this point that the memory dissolves and I go directly to the note and the bottle of pills. What happened between these two moments can't really be described anyway. D. H. Lawrence[51] notwithstanding.

Sometime very late at night, or very early in the morning, I woke up abruptly. It was chilly, and I was lying in bed alone. I was immediately wide awake, aware that there was something wrong. I got out of bed to look for her, moving barefoot out of the bedroom, into the living room.

I found her lying on the couch in her bathrobe, her mouth open. One of the Ted Hugheses was sitting on her chest. There was just enough light coming from the window to see that she was not merely sleeping. I took her pulse and could barely feel it. I slapped her in the face a couple of times, but she didn't react.

The note was on the table beside the wine bottle. Like her poems, it was first draft and to the point.

What a lovely way to die. Thank you. . . . Please take care of Ted Hughes. García Lorca can take care of himself.

I rummaged frantically for the phone, finding it buried in cushions and off the hook, and dialed the operator. When I started to babble, she told me to remain calm. She asked me my name, address, and phone number. I didn't know the phone number. I squinted at the phone in the dark for the number but couldn't read it.

"I don't live here. I'm a taxi driver," I explained, then started screaming, "Would you just send a fucking ambulance!" I shouted the address and hung up.

[51]Sexually challenged English writer (1885–1930) whose overcooked 1928 novel, *Lady Chatterley's Lover,* is a seminal work of early-twentieth-century clitorocentrism.

I went into the bathroom, looking for the pills. There was nothing in the wastebasket or in the medicine cabinet. I looked all over the apartment until I found a pill bottle in the trash under the kitchen sink. It had contained one hundred Seconal, and it was empty.

I ran back to the living room, picked her up, and tried to walk with her, but she was dead weight in my arms. I dialed the operator again and told her about the Seconal. It was a different operator, and she had no idea what I was talking about. While I was trying to explain things to her, the door buzzer rang. I didn't know where the button was to let someone in, so I ran out into the hallway.

It wasn't until I opened the door to let in the paramedics that I realized I was naked. They seemed completely unfazed. I led them into the apartment. They took one look at her and went to work. While one of them gave her CPR, the other had a stethoscope out and was listening to her breathing. I told him about the Seconal. He asked me how many had been left in the bottle before she took it, and I said I didn't know.

It was clear that I didn't know very much. In the ambulance on the way to the hospital I was asked questions about her medical history, and I told them I had only met her the day before. I didn't even know how old she was.

They took her through the doors of the ER, and that was the last I saw of her for hours. I dozed as well as I could on a bench, surrounded by New York City's shot, beaten, run over, crashed, burned, and OD'd. They just kept dragging their asses in there. It never stopped.

I pestered the nurses for information, but they didn't know anything. Finally, after I had drifted off to sleep, an intern tapped me on the shoulder.

"Mr. Mendoza?"

I shot awake, and he didn't wait for a reply. "Your wife's going to be okay. Another hour and we would have lost her."

I stared at him blankly as the words sank in.

"Can I see her?"

"She's not feeling too well at the moment. We had to pump her stomach. There'll be a psych resident down to talk to you."

"But can I see her?"

"Why don't you wait and talk to the doctor first?" And he walked away.

"Why?" I called after him, but he was gone. As I wandered around looking for a coffee machine, I considered walking out of the hospital, going downtown, and forgetting about Karen Mendoza. But even as this thought occurred to me, I knew that there was no way I was going to walk out on her, just as there had been no way I was going to throw out the poems, or not come back after the first visit or, for that matter, not pick her up that night in the rain.

She was a Karen. And I had woken up in time to save her life. And now that I had saved it, I was, as the Chinese say, responsible for it.

It was almost noon before Dr. Melman showed up. He looked like he was about nineteen and called me Mr. Mendoza too.

Taking me into a relatively quiet corner, he took out a file, glanced at it, then looked at me and said, "You are her . . . ?"

I didn't know what I was, so I didn't say anything.

"Boyfriend?"

"Okay . . ."

"Can you tell me any history? Is this her first suicide attempt? Is she undergoing psychiatric treatment?"

"I just met her."

"I see," he said, in a tone that seemed to say that *that* explained everything.

"Look, I really don't know very much about her except that she's blind and she writes poetry and she lives alone in an apartment on West Ninety-sixth Street."

"Is there any family?"

"I don't know."

Sighing deeply, he put down his file and looked at me as if I were responsible for his inability to fill out his forms.

"We don't have a lot to go on here, do we?"

"She's a poet," I said. "Both of her cats are named Ted Hughes, who was Sylvia Plath's husband, so, you know, maybe that explains something."

They obviously didn't cover modern American poetry in Dr. Melman's medical school because he looked at me blankly. "Sylvia Platt?"

"Pla*th*."

Having reached an impasse, we sat there trying to figure out where to go from there until he closed his file and said, "Well, I suggest we send her upstairs for observation. What do you think?"

"I don't know. What do they do up there?"

"Evaluate her. We need to know whether this is just an isolated attempt or if she's seriously suicidal, don't we?"

I nodded, without conviction. I didn't know what anybody needed to know at that point. I had the impression that Dr. Melman's biggest problem was what to write on the form attached to his clipboard.

Sometime in the middle of the afternoon, I was finally permitted to see her. They had her in a holding area, in a corridor off the ER, which was nothing more than a few gurneys with curtains around them.

She was awake, staring at the ceiling, her eyes deader than usual. I brought a chair over and sat down.

"You have to get me out of here. Right away," she said, recognizing my scent before I had said a word.

"How are you feeling?"

"Are there any nurses around here?"

She beckoned for me to move closer. I leaned in and she whispered, "They want to put me upstairs in a locked ward. I can't go there."

"Did you talk to the doctor?"

"They don't know anything. Please. Take me home. Right now. I can't be locked in. I refuse to be locked in."

"Maybe you ought to talk to a doctor . . ."

"I told you. They don't know anything. Please . . . I have to get out of here."

I looked around and saw the bathrobe she had arrived in lying at the foot of the bed. She was wearing a flimsy hospital gown. It was cold outside.

"Let's go," she said, grabbing the bathrobe and putting it on.

I helped her out of bed. Groggy from whatever they had given her, she leaned heavily on my arm. I wrapped her blanket around her over the bathrobe, and we moved out of the cubicle, down the hall, and into the main ER.

Nobody stopped us, nobody said anything to us. Not even the cop at the door, who was asleep on his feet. We walked right past him and out into the glaring cold sunlight of the winter afternoon.

It was four o'clock, shift change, and it took some time to get a cab. I put my arms around her to keep her warm. People walked past us, not batting an eyelash. This was New York. You saw people wrapped in blankets all the time.

The cabbie was a Haitian with a heavy foot. When I asked him to slow down, he said something to me in patois, probably, Go fuck yourself. I stiffed him.

She didn't have her key with her, and we had to ring the super, Mr. Edelman, to let us into her apartment.

"You don't look so good, sweetheart," he said.

"You wouldn't either, Sol, if you just had your stomach pumped."

"So how come you want to go do that?"

"I'm trying to lose weight."

Ted Hughes did not seem particularly excited to see her. They didn't even bother getting up from the couch. I put her to bed, tucking her in like a child.

While she slept I rummaged around the apartment looking for concrete information about her. There was nothing inside her purse to help me—no social security card, no credit cards. I looked for a phone book, a diary, shopping lists, anything. There were books in the apartment, mostly fiction and poetry, but none in Braille.

I reread her poems. As if there were a clue to her inside those little jeweled land mines; they would blow up in your face if you looked too closely at them. The poems were a camouflage. You wouldn't find her underneath the words. She'd be long gone by the time you finished reading them.

Sometime around midnight she woke. I made her tea and toast.

She took a sip of tea, then touched my cheek and said, "You're tired. Come lie down beside me."

I lay down, my head in her lap, and she sang me a Spanish lullaby. Her voice was breathy, a little off-key, but there was a sweetness to the melody that put me to sleep.

It was turning light again when I woke. My heart caught for a split second, until I reached over and felt her beside me, warm and breathing peacefully.

The next time I woke the sun was up and I could smell food cooking in the kitchen. I wandered out of the bedroom, sleep in my eyes, and saw her moving purposefully around her small kitchen preparing bacon and eggs.

We sat at the small wooden table and ate breakfast, both of us ravenous. García Lorca must have returned sometime that morning. He was lying at her feet, snoring.

"There're a lot of questions I want to ask you," I said.

"You won't like the answers."

"How do you know?"

"I know."

"What are you afraid of?"

"Being locked up."

"I'm not going to lock you up."

She turned her eyes toward mine. What was she seeing? It was as if she were looking right through you to something on the other side.

"Can you see anything at all?"

"Just light and dark. But I know what you look like. I felt you with my hands. I know exactly what you look like."

"How do you write if you can't see what you're writing?"

"You don't write with your eyes."

"How long ago did you lose your vision?"

"No more questions. Read to me. Please."

"What?"

"*Anna Karenina*. Start at the part where she meets Vronsky for the first time."

* * *

I stayed there for a week. I read *Anna Karenina* to her through the short winter afternoons. We took walks, and I described the world to her. I shopped for food. She cooked me omelettes and made me ham and cheese sandwiches.

She grew stronger as each day passed. The suicide attempt receded into the past until it seemed as if it had never happened. She didn't speak about it, and I didn't ask because I knew it was futile to ask her anything.

We lived in a cocoon built for two. It was just the two of us in this little apartment with the cats and the dog, the incense, the music, and Tolstoy.

When I began to get cabin fever, she told me to go away for a day. She assured me she was fine. I gave her my phone number and said I would come back and see her the day after tomorrow. She assured me that if she started having dark thoughts she would call me.

I remember standing at the door and saying good-bye. She was sitting on the couch, Ted Hughes in her lap, her eyes unfocused and looking past me. When she waved, she waved at something two feet to my right.

So I went home, changed my clothes, and called the garage.

"Where were you, Lower Slobbovia?" Manny asked me when I picked up my cab.

She had made me promise not to call her for at least a day, but I did anyway and got a busy signal. I was sure she'd taken the phone off the hook.

I took the cab in at midnight, went back to my apartment, picked up the phone to call her, put it back down.

It was almost dawn before I fell asleep. I slept till one o'clock, then lay in bed thinking about her until it was time to pick up a cab. I would stop off at the Belmore, get something to eat, and then drive up and see her.

It's strange what you remember and what you forget about the books you've read in your life. At some point, undoubtedly during my Russian novel period, when I plowed through Dostoyevsky, Turgenev, Gogol, and Tolstoy, I had read *Anna Karenina*. Rereading it to her, I remembered Anna, Vronsky, Levin, Kitty, the brooding Russian melancholy that floats through it. I remembered everything except the ending.

It wasn't until I was sitting at the Belmore with a bowl of navy bean soup and looked over absently at the front page of the early evening edition of the *Post* lying on the table that it came back to me.

The headline read: WOMAN KILLS HERSELF IN SUBWAY. I grabbed the paper, found the piece on page 2, beside a half-page ad for the Dime Savings Bank.

An unidentified woman threw herself in front of the D train in the 96th Street station at approximately 3:40 A.M. this morning. . . .

I ran every light on the way uptown, parked at a hydrant, and rang her bell, even though I knew she wasn't there. I rang the super's bell, leaning on the button like a lunatic, until Edelman came to the door.

"What are you, some sort of crazy person?"

"I need you to let me into Karen's apartment."

"Why should I let you into her apartment?"

"Because she's not there . . ."

He looked at me like I really *was* crazy. After I ranted about *Anna Karenina* and the suicide in the subway, he let me in and unlocked her apartment door. I walked into the bedroom and found what I knew I would find.

The book was lying on her bed, an envelope as a bookmark. I opened it to the scene she had been reading. The eastbound local from Moscow was approaching Obiralovka. . . . There was a light snow falling . . .

and suddenly she realized what she must do. With a quick, light step she went down the stairs and stopped close to the passing train . . .

The envelope was addressed simply to Vronsky. I unfolded the onionskin paper and read what she had written. As usual, it was short and unrevised.

You arrived too late, my love, and too early. . . . Anna

I sat on the bed, my head in my hands, ignoring Edelman until he finally left. Sometime later two police detectives appeared in the apartment. They asked me questions, to which I didn't know the answers. It was just like at the hospital.

When they asked me if I would identify the body, I said I wasn't up to it. Edelman went with them, while I lay down on the bed and curled up into a ball until I was woken by Ted Hughes. I went into the kitchen, found the cat food, and fed them. Then I left the apartment, took the cab in early, and told Manny that my grandmother had died.

* * *

Years later, many years later, a therapist told me that it was time to forgive myself for having left Karen Mendoza alone that night. Without professional help, maybe even with it, she would have killed herself sooner or later, he assured me.

"How do *you* know?" I asked him.

My penance was Ted Hughes. I took them home with me, along with the notebook of poems and the copy of *Anna Karenina.* They lived with me for a couple of months before I found them a hippie commune on Avenue D, where presumably they led long, happy lives amid the marijuana and the Ravi Shankar.

As far as García Lorca was concerned, he was nowhere to be found. I checked her apartment every day for two weeks, but he never showed up. I assume he was gunned down by fascists on Columbus Avenue. Early in the morning. In the rain.

VIII
ENTROPY IN QUEBEC

Entropy represents the thermodynamic measure of the amount of energy unavailable for useful work in a system undergoing temperature change.
>   —Second law of thermodynamics

J ust what I was doing in Quebec City in the winter of 1977 is not easy to explain. You don't spend the months of December through March forty-six degrees, forty-nine minutes north of the equator without a good reason. I didn't really have one until I met Karen Levesque. And even then, in spite of the way her eyes went crooked and her neck quivered when I kissed her, I probably had a better reason to head south. But I didn't. I stuck out the winter in a garret apartment on the rue Ste. Anne, was interrogated by the FLQ,[52] delivered pizzas in snowstorms, and had one of the more exotic sexual experiences of my life.

I had not been planning on spending the winter there. I was actually en route to Vancouver when I arrived in Quebec City in early December with the idea of staying a couple of days, having a look around, and then heading west. But after a few hours of walking

---

[52]Front de Libération du Québec, radical French Canadian separatist movement, active in the 1960s and '70s, that may or may not still be in operation; if it is, I would like them to know that my connection with the Montcalm Club d'Echecs in 1977 was entirely circumstantial.

through the old city, with its twisted little streets and seventeenth-century architecture, I decided to stay for a while.

To be perfectly honest, it wasn't the architecture or the charm. It was the women. The city was full of good-looking women. And much like the women of Togo, the women of Quebec had the French touch in wardrobe and manner, the little *je ne sais quoi* that I had grown to appreciate.

And to be even more perfectly honest, it wasn't only that the women were attractive; it was that they were abundant. In fact, it seemed as if there were no men in the city. It was like wartime, with all the men away fighting at the front. In this case, however, the men weren't away fighting at the front but away working in Ontario, since there weren't a lot of jobs in Quebec at the time. Thus I became a de facto beneficiary of the severe unemployment problem in Quebec.

You had to like your chances in Quebec in the 1970s.

I had been working on another novel for some time. Four hundred pages in, I had to admit to myself that I had very little idea where it was heading. The novel was entitled *The Second Law of Thermodynamics*,[53] and purported, at least when I had started writing it, to be about the entropy of human existence. The universe was running down. Things were falling apart. Energy was being dissipated. That type of thing.

In any event, there seemed to be no reason I couldn't work on the book in Quebec as well as in Vancouver, and so I decided to unpack the Olivetti portable and find a place to live.

What I found was a one-room apartment, bathroom in the hall, on the top floor of an old building on the rue Ste. Anne in the Up-

[53]Film rights available through International Creative Management, Beverly Hills, California.

per Town. From my tiny window you could see the green patina of the towers of the Château Frontenac and the docks at Lévis across the river.

During those first few days in early December, I wandered the streets, the collar of my worn leather jacket up against the icy wind off the St. Lawrence, looking for some respite from the morass of *The Second Law of Thermodynamics.*

I knew enough French from my days in Togo to get around, though it took a while for my ear to adjust to the singsong nasality of the Québecois version of the language. But it didn't take long for my eye to adjust to the women. There were so many of them, on the streets, in the shops, their heads wrapped in berets and wool stocking caps, their cheeks as rosy as tart apples. They would return my smiles, or the few lines I would utter in my Togolese-accented French, but none of them invited me home for pea soup in front of the fire.

Eventually, I wandered into the Café Rimbaud[54]—a coffeehouse on a little hilly street off the rue St. Jean. It was dark with crude wooden tables, candles, Georges Brassens music mixed with Jefferson Airplane. On the wall over the fireplace was a faded portrait of the eponymous poet looking like his foot was hurting him. I would sit there with a book, drink espresso, play chess, and smile at the women who frequented the place.

Karen Levesque didn't smile at me. She wasn't a smiler. She was a waitress who worked the night shift and wore bulky sweaters, short skirts, and dark panty hose. Her hair was tied up in a bun on top, off her neck. It was a superb neck.

---

[54]Arthur Rimbaud, French Symbolist poet (1854–1891) who was shot in the foot by Verlaine in a lovers' quarrel in a hotel room in Brussels and survived only to have his other leg amputated eighteen years later in Marseilles.

I am not a vampire, nor do I have any tendencies in that direction, but I am a great aficionado of necks. I spent a fair amount of time fantasizing about Karen Levesque's neck. When she bent over my table to deposit a cup of espresso, I had to restrain myself from reaching out and caressing her neck or, worse, licking it.

After a while I began to notice that she would shave a dollar or so off my check every night. Invariably she would charge me for only three coffees instead of the four or five I had drunk.

Either she was interested or I looked like a charity case. It's true that I had very little money and would, in fact, soon have to look for a job. But how would she have known this? My wardrobe of worn leather jacket, threadbare scarf, fishing sweater, and jeans was no worse than the norm for the Café Rimbaud.

My 1969 VW Beetle was parked on a street near the Ursuline Convent, buried in mounds of snow. You could barely see the radio antenna emerging from the drifts. I decided to dig it out one day in order to offer Karen Levesque a ride home after work.

I drove it to the Café Rimbaud, parking it illegally on the sidewalk outside next to all the other illegally parked cars. I spent the evening playing chess with Etienne LaCroix, a thin, balding cynic in his late twenties with a day job in the social security office and the founder of the Montcalm Club d'Echecs,[55] a chess club which met in a room in back of an all-night bakery on the rue Père Marquette to play chess from midnight till dawn.

Before midnight, Etienne LaCroix often hung out at the Café Rimbaud with his chess set, looking for action. I very rarely beat him, but when I did, as I did that night, he took it very badly. He in-

---

[55]Marquis de Montcalm de Saint-Véran, French general (1712–1759) whose military ineptitude led to the British victory at the Battle of Quebec in 1759 and sealed the fate of French colonial expansion in North America.

sisted on going back over each move and isolating the exact moment when he'd made the crucial error and then waving his hand dismissively and sighing. *"Mais, tout à fait, tout à fait . . ."*

To my disappointment, Karen Levesque was wearing a turtleneck sweater that night. Which may have accounted for my ability to concentrate on the chessboard and advance a pawn past Etienne LaCroix's defenses to win the game.

She served us our coffee perfunctorily, and, judging from her demeanor, I began to regret having spent two hours with a snow shovel that afternoon. Still, after Etienne LaCroix had departed for the bakery, I asked her if I could drive her home after work.

She shrugged. It was a very Gallic shrug, the type of shrug that Isabelle Huppert[56] would give you if you asked her to go to bed with you. It was a shrug that meant: What difference does it make to me? Maybe I'll go to bed with you and maybe I won't, but don't expect me to jump up and down about it.

Karen Levesque seemed even less enthusiastic when I chipped away the ice that had formed on the passenger door and ushered her into the frozen Volkswagen. Conversation was sparse during the treacherous ride down the narrow icy streets that led to the Lower Town.

"Ça va?"

"Oui."

"Il fait froid."

"Oui."

Her apartment was on the top floor of a two-story wood-frame house on a bleak street near a maple syrup factory. The cloying

---

[56]French actress noted for her extraordinary *froideur.* The late Roger Vadim reportedly said about her, "You could fuck her for three days straight and she would never smile once."

smell of fermented sap hung in the air. The car heater didn't work, and we sat in front of the house, shivering, as I waited for her to invite me up.

"*Tu veux monter?*" she said finally, in the same tone of voice that she would ask you if you wanted another coffee.

I followed her up the rickety steps and into a kitchen that didn't feel a whole lot warmer than my car. There was a light coming from the hallway, illuminating the beige and cream checkered wallpaper and linoleum floor.

She didn't turn the light on in the kitchen. She didn't take off her coat, or her gloves. She just stood in the middle of the room like she was waiting for a bus. I stood opposite her, still shivering.

It was too cold to just stand there and do nothing. So we grabbed each other and kissed. It was a very long kiss. I tasted jasmine tea and cigarettes on her breath. There were a lot of clothes between us, jackets and sweaters, scarves and gloves.

Eventually we came up for air. I liked the way her eyes looked, as if they were banked by a low fire beneath her eyeballs. My fingers reached the top button of her coat and slowly began to unbuttoned it. Her neck was hidden beneath the turtleneck. Slowly, I slid the turtleneck down to reveal it in its superb nudity.

Then with one hand under her open coat, I began to kiss her neck. It tasted as delicious as I had imagined. She must have liked it because her eyes were slipping out of focus.

A cat suddenly came into the kitchen and leaped up on a counter. It was a moment of distraction, and in that moment of distraction she apparently had second thoughts about whatever it was that we were going to do because she pulled away and told me that I had to go.

It was my turn to ask *pourquoi?*

"Parce que."

The classic nonanswer answer. I didn't want to leave, and I sensed that she really didn't want me to leave, but I didn't like the no-no-no-yes routine and so I said, *"C'est dommage,"* and left.

* * *

I stayed away from the Café Rimbaud for a few days to make her suffer for sending me back out into the tundra at 1:00 A.M. with an erection. But to judge by her manner when I saw her again, she hadn't suffered a great deal. She was businesslike and correct when she took my order, even asked me how I was, but she didn't linger at the table.

She did, however, wear a sweater that fully revealed her neck. Was this just enticement? Was she rubbing it in? Or was she playing a cat and mouse game with me?

A little before one o'clock, I was just about to leave when Karen Levesque asked me if I had my car with me. I told her it was back buried under the snow. She asked me if I would walk her to the bus stop after she closed up.

"Pourquoi pas?" I said, trying to match the indifference with which she had made the invitation.

I helped her stack the chairs on the tables and then walked out with her into the frozen streets. It had snowed earlier, as it always seemed to do at night in Quebec City that winter, and the snowplows were creeping through the streets like giant insects, heaving large drifts on top of the cars belonging to people too poor to have their cars garaged.

We walked to the bus stop without a word and then stood in the shelter and indulged in another furious vertical necking session before the bus arrived. We were both breathing hard when she broke away and got on the bus. She did not wave good-bye to me through the steaming window.

I walked back home through the white streets feeling like I was in high school again, back at first base. There was something painfully nostalgic about walking home through the cold with a dull ache in my scrotum. I thought about all those girls, Karens and non-Karens alike, who had left me stranded out there on the base paths.

The odor of baking bread snapped me out of my nostalgia. I was passing the Montcalm Club d'Echecs and decided to stop in. Entering the bakery through the side entrance that gave on the parking lot, I found myself in the small storage room beside the room with the ovens, where Etienne LaCroix was playing with Jean-Marie Morin while three other chess freaks watched.

Nobody said hello to me. Nobody even acknowledged my presence. They were all focused on the chessboard. I walked over, opening my coat against the heat from the ovens, and watched a nasty endgame of attrition being played out.

I had played chess with some of these people at the Café Rimbaud for hours and yet knew practically nothing about them. They all presumably had day jobs, but I didn't know what they were.

I would run into one of them weeks after playing a game, a game I had long ago forgotten, and he would say to me, "Remember that isolated passed pawn I had against you, when you had opened the queen bishop's file?" I didn't remember it; in fact, I had forgotten about it five minutes after the game was over. But he hadn't forgotten about it. *Au contraire.* He had been carrying it around with him for weeks, stored in some sort of bottomless file cabinet containing past games and positions. And he would set the pieces up in exactly the same position and want to replay the game.

I had been standing watching the game for about ten minutes when two men came in from the street. They were wearing stocking caps and pea jackets. They didn't look like chess players to me. They didn't have that absent, preoccupied, unhealthy look of people who spent the majority of their time staring at chessboards.

As soon as they walked in, the atmosphere of the place changed. Suddenly all eyes were on them, and their eyes were on me, as if to say, Who is this guy? Though not a word was spoken, I got the impression that I was not supposed to be there.

I uttered a quick *au revoir* and took off, trudging back through the snow to my apartment with the odor of baking bread in my nostrils and the sense memory of Karen Levesque on my lips.

* * *

When my financial situation became too precarious to ignore, I scoured the skimpy want ads for gainful employment. There was very little in the way of jobs to be had in Quebec City and even less for an American without working papers.

But for a foreigner with his own car, there was a job delivering pizzas for a place called Le Pizza à Go Go on the Avenue Jacques-Cartier. So I dug the VW out of the drifts again and went down for an interview. A short, dapperly dressed Greek named Heraclitus Zotakis explained that the job involved delivering hot pizzas before they got cold. It required sharp driving skills to get the pizzas there before they cooled in the arctic temperature of wintertime Quebec.

Heraclitus Zotakis did not realize he was dealing with an ex–New York cabbie until I had taken him for a harrowing ride up and down the narrow icy streets of the old city. White-faced and a little shaky, he hired me on the spot. When I asked him what the pay was, he told me it was 25 percent of the price of the pizza and tips.

Two nights a week, business was especially brisk. On Wednesday and Saturday nights *La Soirée du Hockey* was televised. The entire city sat home and watch the Canadiens play, and a lot of them ordered take-out pizza.

On those two nights I sped around town with a big Le Pizza à Go Go sign attached to the roof of my car. I'd run up and down stairs with my pizzas, impatient to get paid and be on my way. If I arrived during a *jeux à cinq*,[57] however, I would be made to wait two minutes, standing in the doorway with my rapidly cooling pizza, until the Canadiens had either scored or survived the one-man disadvantage.

My job at Le Pizza à Go Go kept me away from the Café Rimbaud six nights a week. When I showed up on Monday, my night off, Karen Levesque and I had our usual conversation.

"*Ça va?*"

"*Oui.*"

"*Il fait froid.*"

"*Oui.*"

She was above asking me where I had been or, more to the point, how I could have gone an entire week without seeing her. And I wasn't going to tell her. But when she saw my car parked outside the Café Rimbaud, she asked me if I would drive her home after work.

I didn't even hesitate. Why play hard to get at this point?

As usual, we drove in silence down the hill in my car, pungent with mozzarella cheese and onions, to her apartment. I hadn't even turned off the ignition before she put her hand on my thigh. We started to kiss with the usual passion, and as my hand reached

---

[57]Power play.

down to caress her neck, her hand reached down to caress me in that special place that is guaranteed to get a man's attention.

I was now, to put it oxymoronically, putty in her hands. I followed her blindly up the stairs, and we were immediately engaged in very heavy vertical petting in the freezing kitchen.

I asked her, hoarsely, where the bedroom was. She put her finger to my lips and shook her head. As I started to protest, she unzipped my fly.

Vertical or not, I wasn't going to look a blow job in the mouth, so I closed my eyes and pretended we were on the beach in Tahiti and not in the cold kitchen of an apartment in lower Quebec City with beige and cream checkered wallpaper and the ugliest linoleum I had ever seen.

When I started to make noise, she reached up with her free hand and covered my mouth. I didn't know why she did this until I heard sounds coming from the other room. Someone was calling her name. It was a woman's voice.

Hurriedly she pushed me toward the door. Before I knew it, I was back out in the cold, my fly still open, stumbling down the stairs in the frigid night air.

I drove home in a fury. This was worse than getting caught at third base. This was getting picked off. In the bottom of the ninth, bases loaded, two outs.

I was still fuming when I got home that night and deposited my car in a snowbank across from the apartment. I walked up the six flights of stairs, unlocked the door, and found two men sitting at my kitchen table, eating slices of cold pizza from my refrigerator.

"*Bonsoir,*" one of them said.

I was trying to form the sentence *What the fuck are you doing in my apartment?* in French when the other one said, "Sit down, make yourself at home," in English.

I sat down and was offered a cigarette. I shook my head, then looked from one to the other and realized that they were the two men who had walked into the Montcalm Club d'Echecs at one in the morning a few weeks back. Even with pizza slices in their hands, they looked menacing.

They ate their pizza, checked my refrigerator for beer and, finding none, had to content themselves with tap water.

"We are going to ask you some question," the English-speaking one said.

"Why?"

"Because we are interested to know who you are."

"What if I don't want to answer them?"

"Why not? They are not difficult question."

There was a brief interchange in very guttural French Canadian, of which I understood only a few words. Then the English-speaking one asked me what I was doing in Quebec.

I told him I was writing a novel about the second law of thermodynamics and working as a pizza deliverer.

He stared at me good and hard. I don't think he was aware that the universe was running down or, for that matter, gave much of a shit.

"You are jerking my chain?"

"It's *yanking* my chain. And no, I'm not."

"How well do you know Etienne LaCroix?"

"Not well at all. I play chess with him occasionally."

"What were you doing that night at the bakery?"

"Warming up from the cold."

"That's all?"

"That's all."

"Don't yank my brain."

"It's chain. Yank my *chain*."

I took a piece of paper and was about to spell it for him when they abruptly got up from the table and headed for the door.

"Thank you for the pizza."

"It's okay. I'm in the business."

*   *   *

The next day at nine in the morning, I had more visitors. These visitors knocked at least. I staggered to the door in my underwear and discovered Karen Levesque and a tall, thin woman with very short hair standing there.

"On peut entrer?"

I stepped back, and they entered the apartment, sat down at the kitchen table, and lit cigarettes.

"C'est mon amie Clothilde. Elle parle anglais," Karen Levesque said.

I nodded at Clothilde, who said, "Hi."

"Hi," I responded.

"I'm from Halifax," Clothilde explained. "But I was born in Trois-Rivières."

I offered them some instant coffee and put the kettle on. As I was doing this, I tried to clear my head and figure out what the woman I had been having unconsummated sexual adventures with was doing in my kitchen at nine in the morning with another woman. I wasn't sure if this was the same voice I had heard last night at Karen Levesque's apartment. Clothilde cleared that up quickly.

"Karen and I live together."

"Uh-huh."

"We are lovers."

Of course. It all suddenly made sense. The stand-up, nonpenetrative sex; the bedroom I never saw; the voice the previous night. But what were they doing here? And what about all that moaning and groaning on Karen Levesque's part during our necking sessions?

I spooned out some instant coffee, brought the cups over to the table, and sat down.

"We'd like to invite you to dinner," Clothilde said.

"Thank you."

"Tomorrow night."

"I have to work tomorrow night."

"When do you finish?"

"Midnight."

"We can have dinner then," she said. "At midnight."

I shrugged, Isabelle Huppert-like. *Pourquoi pas?*

Clothilde then asked me some questions. They were not at all like the questions that the two goons from the Montcalm Club d'Echecs had asked me the night before. She wanted to know how old I was, what my astrological sign was, if my parents were still alive, and how my health was.

Of course, I should have figured it out. But as I've said, I was not running on all cylinders that winter.

After they left, I went back to sleep and didn't awake till the middle of the afternoon. I showered, shaved, dressed, and took a long walk along the esplanade above the St. Lawrence thinking about how everything that had happened that winter had happened according to the second law of thermodynamics. My life was inefficient. I was not engaged in useful work. I was losing heat.

I showed up at Le Pizza à Go Go at 5:30. It was a Wednesday night. The Canadiens were playing the Maple Leafs, and everybody in Quebec City was home watching the game. I ran around like a madman with my pizzas, up and down the stairs. The Canadiens were winning big. The tips were good.

By the time I quit, I was exhausted and no longer hungry. I had inhaled a lot of tomato and mozzarella. A midnight supper did not seem very appealing. But I showed up at their apartment at 12:30, as I knew I would.

Clothilde came to the door wearing studded jeans, a fluffy sweater, and patent leather boots. She smiled and invited me in.

The apartment was warm and redolent of food and incense. There was a robust fire going in the fireplace and low lighting. Pachelbel's Canon[58] oozed from the stereo. I took off my leather jacket and gloves. Clothilde brought me a glass of wine.

In the corner of the living room was a dining alcove with a candlelit table and three place settings. Clothilde and I sat down on the sofa, sipped our wine, and had a pleasant conversation about the best way to tune up a Volkswagen. In the middle of this conversation, Karen Levesque made her appearance.

She was wearing a black sheath dress, stockings, and heels. There was a simple strand of pearls around her exquisite neck, bracelets on her wrists and around one of her ankles. She looked stunning.

When she leaned down to kiss me on both cheeks, I inhaled the exotic fragrance of a perfume more evocative of Bali or Singapore than of Quebec City in February.

She sat down beside me, and Clothilde got up and went into the kitchen to see about dinner.

"*Ça va?*"

"*Oui.*"

---

[58]Johann Pachelbel (1653–1706), German composer whose cloying Canon, though fresh and innovative in the seventeenth century, when it was written, as well as in the 1970s, when I first heard it, is now played at every other wedding and avant-garde bar mitzvah, usually by a flutist standing on a cliff overlooking an ocean as the sun sets.

"*Il fait froid.*"

"*Oui.*"

We listened to the Pachelbel Canon in silence, sipped our wine, until Clothilde summoned us to the table. I sat opposite Karen Levesque. Clothilde served an excellent boeuf bourguignon with home-baked bread and perfectly parboiled *haricot verts*.

As I ate and drank and listened to the music, I admired Karen Levesque. In the candlelight, her face embellished with just a soupçon of eye makeup, just enough to bring out the melancholy of her green-gray eyes, she looked like a heroine out of Zola.

I tried not to think about what was happening. Because I knew that if I thought about it, I might start to have serious reservations, and I was feeling too good at the moment to have reservations. There was a soft inevitability about it all that I didn't want to interfere with.

So I ate and drank, chatted amiably with Clothilde about rear-mounted, air-cooled engines and how they provided good traction in the snow, and waited for things to unfold.

We had dessert in front of the fire. Home-baked apple tart with vanilla ice cream. Karen Levesque spoon-fed the ice cream to me. She lay in front of me on cushions, her neck glowing in the fire-light.

Between the wine, the fire, and the food, we were all getting very warm.

"*Il fait chaud.*"

"*Oui.*"

Clothilde removed her sweater. She was not wearing a bra. Her nipples were a very deep red. Karen Levesque rubbed her lover's nipples lightly until they hardened. Then she reached for me and rubbed me lightly until I hardened.

I decided to follow their lead, wherever it went. What could be the worst thing that would happen? I thought. It was the last time I thought.

They took off the rest of their clothes, and then they undressed me together. I watched their foreplay, fascinated. I was both an observer and a participant. When Karen Levesque arched her back, her neck was irresistible, and I kissed it. It tasted of Burgundy and perfumed beads of perspiration.

She had a pale blue tattoo of a spidery tree that threaded up from the insides of her thighs over her belly. Her lover had a matching tattoo on her lower buttocks that ran down and disappeared between her legs. I imagined that when they were locked together in love the branches would intertwine.

It was Clothilde who took me and put me inside her lover, wet from her ministrations. And then, as soon as I was inside, she moved on top of me and wrapped her arms and legs around my sides so that they reached down beneath Karen Levesque.

I was sandwiched between the two women, one on top and one below. Clothilde was not heavy, but she was strong. I could feel the strength in her arms and legs as she moved her face down across my shoulder and kissed her lover on the lips.

"Baise-la bien!" she whispered hoarsely into my ear. She moved rhythmically on top of me as if we were horse and rider cantering across a field.

My lips stayed buried in Karen Levesque's neck as Clothilde rode me hard on the backstretch, urging me on, slapping my hip with the palm of her hand.

Pachelbel was building to a crescendo. We were neck and neck in the homestretch. It was going to be close. The three of us were screaming and moaning in different languages, dripping wet in Burgundy sweat.

I don't remember who crossed the finish line first, Pachelbel or me. I think it was a photo finish. All three of us collapsed into a heap, and then Clothilde, not very gently, peeled me off her lover and fell into her arms. I lay by their side as the two of them whispered endearments into each other's ears.

They fell asleep, as if I weren't even there. Soon they were both snoring peacefully. Not bothering to disturb them, I redressed and let myself out.

Fuck it, I said to myself. Maybe someday they'll send me a picture.

*   *   *

They didn't send me a picture. To this day I am not sure whether Karen Levesque conceived my child that night of the boeuf bourguignon and Pachelbel Canon. But I suspect not. Because when I dropped into the Café Rimbaud a few days later, she did not look at all happy.

"*Ça va?*" I asked her.

"*Non.*"

"*Pourquoi?*"

She welled up a little bit, shook her head, and said, "*Ça n'a pas marché.*"

"What?"

But she wouldn't explain just what it was that hadn't worked.

And so that's how it turned out. I had been a hired sperm gun. And I didn't even get my man.

In the days that followed I thought about the necking sessions, the blow job interruptus, all that heat radiating through all that clothing. Was it all some sort of elaborate foreplay, designed from the very beginning to lure me into the after-dinner love sandwich? Or was Karen Levesque sincerely conflicted? Was she a lesbian who liked men, or a straight woman who liked women, or just a woman who liked having sex standing up in the cold? Or was it just one of life's entropic moments that is best left unexplained?

And then, as if things weren't entropic enough, one day in early March I opened the newspaper and saw on the front page the photo of the two men who had visited me late at night at my apartment. They had been arrested when a cache of bombs blew up in the bakery on the rue Père Marquette. Standing beside them in the photo was Etienne LaCroix. All three of them were active members of a militant cell of the Front de Libération du Québec, the article claimed, and the bakery, masquerading as the Montcalm Club d'Echecs, was a front for their operation. In the back room, where the flour was stored, the police had found enough dynamite to blow up half the city. Authorities were looking to speak with other members of the chess club and their known associates.

By noon I had packed up the Volkswagen and was heading south to the Vermont border. It had been a hard winter. I had delivered pizzas for food and gas money. I had nearly gotten blown up playing chess. I was wanted for questioning by the RCMP. I had been seduced and sandwiched by two women for the purpose of appropriating my sperm.

Six women to every man, and the only time I had gotten laid was as a stud horse. Talk about entropy.

Every now and then I think about that winter of 1977 and about Karen Levesque. I wonder whether she and Clothilde lived happily ever after. And then I remember her beautiful crazy eyes, her hot breath on my neck, and I close my eyes very tightly until her image has vanished, and all that is left is snow flurries on the screen. And the smell of pizza.

IX
THE SCRABBLE HUSTLER

*K*aren *number nine* made her living taking showers in a glass booth mounted on a stage in a construction workers' bar on Canal Street. But I didn't know that when I met her. At the time I thought she was just a good Scrabble player with beautiful cheekbones.

It was at a party in the Village, at the apartment of a friend of a friend, somebody in publishing, sometime in the late seventies. There was a lot of booze floating around and a lot of Judy Collins and James Taylor, and a fair amount of onion dip. It was deep summer, hot and humid, and the sliding glass door was open to the terrace, where she stood, a large gin and tonic condensing in her hand.

My first take on her was an assistant editor at a publishing house, the kind of woman who collected writers and had short, unhappy affairs with the men in her office. None of this was true, of course, but that's what I was thinking when I wandered over and said something probably a tad pretentious.

She looked me over carefully, taking in the pressed khakis and the madras sport jacket, and must have figured that it all didn't really add up. It didn't. I had a very slippery purchase on the publishing business, consisting of a job writing and editing what is euphemistically referred to as adult fiction.

I was working at Midworld Books,[59] a subsidiary of a subsidiary

---

[59]Not its real name.

of a mainstream publishing house, which, because of its large legal staff, will have to remain nameless. For eight hours a day I sat in a small office in the back of a large office copyediting manuscripts from Midworld's stable of authors; at night I moonlighted writing them myself under the nom de plume of Vanessa Vellacruz.

It was down and dirty: $800 for 30,000 words, one sex act per chapter, lots of adjectives. Midworld retained the copyright, not that any of us who wrote these books wanted anything to do with them after we delivered the manuscripts and got our money. It was essentially industrial piecework.

Strictly speaking, then, I was a published author, and I undoubtedly tried to project that image when I sidled up to her, looked out at the inky black and white city, and said whatever it was I said.

She said whatever it was she said, and we engaged in some repartee until I made some tangential reference to Scrabble and she told me she had a portable set in her shoulder bag and wondered if I might be interested in a game.

Now if there's one person you shouldn't play Scrabble with, it's a person who travels with her own set in her shoulder bag. You wouldn't play poker with someone who took a deck of cards out of his pocket, would you? But between my ego and my libido, I was an easy mark.

We found a relatively quiet corner in the living room and set up the board. As the party degenerated around us, James Taylor giving way to John Denver, we played cutthroat Scrabble until it was that time when people began taking a last look around the room to determine if there was anybody that they had overlooked who was worth making a final run at as a prelude to going home and having impersonal late 1970s pre-AIDS sex with.

But we were focused on a tense endgame, separated by a few points and trying to play out our tiles on a tight board. I was stuck with an *i,* an *e,* a *t,* and a *u.* My only chance to win was to play out and stick her with the *q.* She sat back in her chair, an expression of incipient triumph on her face.

I took a moment to appreciate how attractive she was. She had high, Slavic cheekbones and very smooth dark skin. The tops of her breasts sloped down gracefully into the off-the-shoulder peasant blouse she wore. As if that weren't enough of a distraction, she wore the type of perfume that was subtle enough to be almost subliminal, which made you think about it even more.

"Nice game," she said, with the noblesse oblige of a gracious winner.

"What makes you think it's over?"

"What are you going to do with your *u?*"

Frankly I couldn't decide whether I wanted more to beat her in Scrabble or to sleep with her.

Most men don't think about small, inlaid-jeweled sewing baskets when they're in heat. Those wires generally run through entirely different circuits. But somehow at that moment, as I was imagining what it would be like to caress her cheekbones, I saw it in front of my eyes. It was a word that you didn't use very often in the course of your life, unless you happened to be an eighteenth-century European noblewoman who sewed on those long winter nights while her husband was off fighting the War of the Spanish Succession and kept her sewing needles in an *etui.*

I laid the tiles down, taking pains to avoid the triumphal sweep of the wrists that obnoxious Scrabble players employ after a particularly impressive move.

To her credit, she did not ask me what the word meant. She knew what the word meant. But she claimed it wasn't a legitimate Scrabble word.

"It's French."

"In origin," I rebutted, "but it has entered the language. I mean, what else do you call the box you keep your sewing needles in?"

"The box you keep your sewing needles in."

We tracked down the host to ask for a dictionary. He was draped over a tall redhead in black leather pants and spiked heels and claimed he didn't have a dictionary anywhere in the apartment.

"How can you not have a dictionary in your apartment?" she asked, in a tone of voice that implied that not having a dictionary in your apartment was like not having a bathroom.

But our host was already directing the redhead toward the bedroom in small, decisive steps and did not reply.

So we left the party with the game unresolved. As far as I was concerned, resolved or not, the hotly contested Scrabble game was an aphrodisiac. And I must have implied something to that effect.

"You have to beat me in Scrabble first," she said, hailing a passing cab. As she got into the taxi, I said, "Can I call you?"

"Sure," she said.

It wasn't until her cab turned up Sixth Avenue that I realized I didn't know her name, let alone her phone number.

*   *   *

I thought about her a lot during the days after the party, as I bluepenciled misplaced modifiers by day (*Hot and throbbing, he stuffed his engorged member into her foaming lava pit*) and wrote clean, graceful, well-turned priapic prose at night.

Vanessa Vellacruz was working on her fifth book, entitled *Arousing Audrey.*[60] It was a picaresque, *Moll Flanders*–like saga of a girl

[60]Not to be confused with *Abusing Audrey,* the working title of the author's fourth novel, subsequently changed to *Abbreviating Ernie* and published by Villard in 1997. Film rights available through International Creative Management, Beverly Hills, California.

who moves into an apartment building in San Diego and evolves from a sweet young thing who wants to be a Delta stewardess to a jaded nymphomaniac cornering washing machine repairmen in the building's laundry room. She has sex twelve times, once every chapter, and always in a different manner. You may think that writing porno novels is easy, but believe me, coming up with more outrageous and inventive ways for human beings to copulate every ten pages can be taxing.

Though the book delivers $800 worth of hard-core sex, it also has a dry subtext that satirizes West Coast culture. Though largely ignored by the literary establishment, *Arousing Audrey* contains elements that may have influenced the Post-Neo-Ironic movement of Southern California novelists[61] that flourished very briefly in Los Angeles in the early 1990s.

Midworld Books was located in an office building on Thirty-fourth Street. You entered the offices of the mainstream publishing house with the large legal staff, walked down a few hallways, past the offices of editors busily making appointments for lunch, and through a door marked NO ADMITTANCE.

Walking through this door branded you as a pornographer, and once the other people in the mainstream publishing house knew you worked at Midworld they didn't want to stand next to you in the elevator, let alone talk to you.

There were only a half dozen of us in the Midworld "division." Besides Harvey, whose fiefdom it was, there was Myrna, his secretary; a numbers cruncher named Arnie; another writer-editor, Gloria; and the gay book specialist, whose name, as far as anybody knew, was Prince Charles, the name under which he wrote his books.

---

[61]Jon Pettermill, Hank De Borgennes, Genevieve Geltenschaung et al.

Prince Charles's biggest seller was a book called *Dennis, Any-one?*[62] It was in its fourteenth printing. I had never read *Dennis, Anyone?* Nor, as far as I knew, had anybody else at Midworld. In-house writers copyedited their own books. Not the best method of quality control, but it kept costs down.

Although I don't think our readers were overly concerned with grammar and spelling, we were each given a style sheet to help us with the kinds of words you didn't find in dictionaries. To do this type of work, it was useful to know, for example, whether *cock-sucking* was one word or hyphenated.[63]

Anyway, the week after the party where I met Karen IX[64] I was busy trying to wrap up *Arousing Audrey.* In order to make the pro-duction deadline, I was working on it in the office during the day as well as at home at night. Audrey had already had sex in the laundry room, the Jacuzzi, her Toyota Corolla, under the sink with the plumber, with her guru, her gynecologist (in the stirrups), and the UPS man. I was looking for something a little less basso profundo, a sort of intermezzo, just before the grand finale—a threesome with two bodybuilders in the apartment complex's weight room. The Scrabble hustler was undoubtedly on my mind because what sprang to mind was Strip Scrabble.

The idea was a little cerebral for my readership, I had to admit. And I knew Harvey would hate it. But the production schedule was so tight, there wasn't a whole lot he could do about it without los-ing a title for the month, and so I went with it.

And writing it (Audrey gets the guy's shorts off with the word *fel-*

---

[62]Eventually made into a film in Paraguay, released under the title *Denis, ¿Por Qué No?*

[63]One word as a gerund, hyphenated as an adjective.

[64]As I must refer to her, because I never knew her last name.

latio on a triple word score) made me think more and more of Karen IX.

I called up the friend who had got me invited to the party. He didn't know who the girl I described was or her phone number, but he gave me the phone number of the guy without a dictionary in his apartment, and I called him.

"*What's* her name?" he asked me.

"I don't know. She's pretty, dark hair, nice cheekbones . . ."

"Cheekbones? You mean, like her ass?"

"No. Her face."

There was silence on the phone for a moment, then he said, "You mean the one with the nice tits?"

"She had very nice breasts. We were playing Scrabble, and she asked you for a dictionary, remember?"

"Oh, *Karen. . . .*"

By this point in my life the Karen phenomenon no longer surprised me.

"She works in a bar on Canal Street, near the Holland Tunnel."

"What's the name of the bar?"

"Ruby's or Rudy's or something. It's full of construction workers. You ought to go down there and catch her act. She takes a shower onstage."

I was convinced he had the wrong girl. I didn't see my Karen, the one who knew what *etui* meant, taking a shower onstage for construction workers. But I didn't have any other leads, so that night I took the subway down to Canal and walked west toward the tunnel.

In the days before Tribeca, Canal Street west of Chinatown was basically bars and factories. Rudy's was a big place with a blinking neon sign that said GIRLS in the window. There was a two-dollar minimum at the door, which bought you a glass of watery tap beer.

You could barely see the stage through the cigarette smoke, and the music was so loud you had to use sign language if you wanted to communicate with anybody. I found a seat at the end of the long bar which circled the stage, upon which a large-breasted woman was prancing around in a spangled G-string, stopping in front of the men who had drooped dollar bills over a rope that ran along the border of the stage. For those guys, she did a private routine before she allowed them to stuff the bills into her G-string; the larger the bill the deeper their hands were allowed to wander.

Pretty standard strip joint procedure. But in the corner of the stage was something I had never seen in one of these places before: a shower stall on wheels. I sat there, watching the strippers parade on and off until, after an hour or so, the construction workers started chanting, "SHOW-ER, SHOW-ER, SHOW-ER!" loudly and in unison, like cheerleaders at a football game.

A voice came over the speakers, "A little hot tonight, guys, isn't it?"

Loud assents.

"Hot enough for a shower?"

"FUCKIN' A! FUCKIN' A! FUCKIN' A!"

Two stagehands rolled the shower stall to the middle of the stage amid tumultuous applause. Then they brought out a chair, a small dressing table with a mirror, and some towels.

"By the way, guys, anybody in particular you want to see take a shower?"

"KA-REN! KA-REN! KA-REN!"

Loud, rhythmic, repetitive incantations. It was like the Nuremberg rallies. As the preparations continued and hoses were connected to the back of the shower stall, the construction workers got more and more excited.

"KA-REN! KA-REN! KA-REN!"

After the disembodied voice stopped asking rhetorical questions over the sound system, the music started up again. But it wasn't canned disco rock. It was that old bump and grind standard, "Also Sprach Zarathustra."[65]

When the frenzy reached a crescendo, Karen IX emerged, wearing a white terry-cloth bathrobe, high heels, and that indispensable accessory for taking a shower, sunglasses.

It was suddenly quiet in the place. Without any acknowledgment to the audience, she sat down at the dressing table, took off the sunglasses, and stared into the mirror.

Very slowly and deliberately, she removed her makeup. The men watched her raptly. It was like they were at some avant-garde Off Broadway theater. When she was finished with her makeup, she tied her hair up on top of her head and then got up and walked toward the shower stall, still not making eye contact with anyone.

Reaching into the shower stall, she turned the water on, adjusting the hot and cold knobs. Then she took off the bathrobe, tossed it over the chair, and got in.

She soaped herself up and shampooed her hair. She did this without self-consciousness, as if she were alone in her apartment taking a shower. She closed her eyes to keep the soap out, rinsed her hair carefully, scrubbed under her armpits.

No one so much as took a sip of beer during the entire performance. All eyes were focused on that shower stall.

Gradually, the glass walls of the stall fogged up, and you began to see less and less of her. It was a sort of reverse striptease: you went from seeing everything to seeing nothing. When she was finished,

---

[65]Work by Richard Strauss (1864–1949), German composer and *Reichsmusikkamer* under the Nazis, banalized by Stanley Kubrick in *2001: A Space Odyssey*.

she turned off the water, stepped out of the shower, walked over and dried herself with one towel, using the other towel to wrap up her wet hair. Then she slipped back into her bathrobe and casually walked off the stage without taking a bow.

For a few seconds the place was dead quiet; then Strauss gave way abruptly to earsplitting disco rock, and we were back in a strip joint. They wheeled the shower stall to the side of the stage, and another girl came out and began her routine.

"Does she take another shower?" I shouted at the guy next to me. He looked at me blankly, and I attempted sign language. When that failed I set off to try to find the manager to get a message to her, but explaining anything to anyone in that noise was impossible. I eventually prevailed on a waitress to give her a note. On a napkin I wrote ETUI and my home and office phone numbers.

* * *

The following morning I was in Harvey's office discussing the Strip Scrabble scene in *Arousing Audrey*. As I had foreseen, Harvey had problems with it.

"The people who read these books don't play Scrabble," he said.

"It's just a device."

"Device? What is it that we're engaged in doing here? We're not doing devices. We're doing whack-off books. And you can't whack off and play Scrabble at the same time, can you?"

At that point Myrna popped her head in to say that I had a personal call. She stressed the word *personal*.

I went to take it in my office, closing the door behind me.

"It's French. I checked the *OED*," was the first thing she said.

It was hard to believe that this was the voice of the woman I had watched, along with a hundred construction workers, taking a shower to "Also Sprach Zarathustra" the night before on Canal Street.

"So how've you been?" I said casually.

"All right."

"You got my note?"

"No. I'm psychic."

"I was thinking . . . maybe we could play some Scrabble tonight."

"What stakes?"

"You want to play for money?"

"Makes it more interesting."

"What if we play for something else?"

"Like what?"

"I don't know . . ."

"You're the writer. Think of something creative."

Thinking creatively, I thought about the woman in my life at the moment. I thought about how she looked in her color-coordinated short shorts and tank top, lying on the deep-pile beige rug of her San Diego condominium, toying with the tiles of her Scrabble set: A, T, F, E, L, I, L. The O was just sitting there, right before the triple word score, waiting to be joined.

"How about Strip Scrabble?" I suggested, in an attempt at nonchalant humor.

There was dead silence on the line. I started to back and fill, preparing to qualify the idea, to distance myself from it with a flippant "just kidding," but before I could get it all out she said, "Every fifty points, the opponent has to take something off?"

"Uh . . . right . . ."

"You're good for at least four hundred points, aren't you?"

"Consistently."

"Wear seven articles of clothing, not counting shoes. When I hit four hundred, you'll be bare-assed. Nine o'clock, okay?"

"Perfect."

She gave me an address in the East Seventies and hung up. I stood in my office staring out onto Sixth Avenue thinking about what I had just done. This wasn't just a case of life imitating art; this was life imitating pornography. Was I out of my fucking mind? I couldn't remember the last time I scored four hundred points.

Well, I said to myself philosophically, the race was not entirely to the swift here, was it? Look what happened to the guy who got scrabbled by Audrey.

For the rest of the day, as I copyedited *Arousing Audrey,* sprinkling a few more torrid adjectives over the already overcooked prose, I contemplated my wardrobe strategy. If I subtracted two for socks, one for underpants, one for pants, one for shirt, I was still two items short.

To get me up to seven, I decided to wear a tie and a belt, with a short-sleeved shirt and lightweight slacks, along with underpants and two socks.

I wondered what she would wear. How would she get up to seven?

* * *

She never got past three. She came to the door wearing only shorts, presumably panties, and a T-shirt, barefoot, no bra. Effectively, she was spotting me four articles of clothing—two hundred points. What supreme hubris!

Her apartment was full of expensive furniture and classy looking artwork. You wouldn't have thought a shower stripper could afford these types of things. She informed me, as if by way of explanation, "Rudy pays me two hundred dollars a night cash. And do you know why?"

I shook my head. I *didn't* know why.

"Because I pack the place. They come to see me, not the G-string stuffers. It adds up, especially when you don't declare it. You don't work for the IRS, do you?"

"Not in this lifetime."

"Want a drink?"

"Sure."

"I've got a bottle of Puligny-Montrachet in the fridge."

So we sat there on cool leather furniture sipping incredibly good white wine, the Scrabble board resting on a sculpted ebony table between us. I tried to make conversation between moves, but she wasn't interested in anything but the game.

It didn't take long to realize that I was in over my head. She had only been toying with me at the party, setting me up for the hustle. This woman was world class. She was decisive, played the board like a piano, and possessed the type of vocabulary you didn't develop by taking showers on Canal Street. In two moves I had lost my tie; one move later and the belt was gone.

By the time I was down to my underwear, all I had gotten off her was her shorts. I had lousy letters. And it didn't help that she was stretched out on the couch in T-shirt and black bikini underwear. Unlike the Volleyball Effect, the Scrabble Effect didn't kick in.

The tiles began to swim in my rack. I was cooked, and I knew it. I was five points short of getting her T-shirt off when she played out with *hinny.*[66]

"Well, you win," I said, a stupid grin on my face.

In the spirit of good sportsmanship I slipped off my Jockeys.

"Well, well, well." She smiled. "Is that a semicolon in your pocket, or are you just happy to see me?"

[66]The offspring of a stallion and a female donkey, as opposed to a *mule,* which is the offspring of a male donkey and a mare.

I took this to be an invitation; in fact, I took the whole Scrabble game to be foreplay. So I got up and moved purposefully toward her. She held up her hand to stop me, like a traffic cop stopping a car from running a light.

"Sorry, but remember our deal? You have to beat me first."

"You're going to hold me to it?"

"You bet."

"It's a shame to waste the rest of the Puligny-Montrachet."

"There's always another night," she said cheerfully, slipping her shorts back on. "How about something to eat?"

"No thank you."

"Don't be a bad sport," she mewed, but I didn't answer. I was dressed and out the door in under three minutes.

I walked all the way downtown, furious. She had taken the term *cocktease*[67] to an entirely new level.

* * *

That night I lay in bed and vowed revenge. I would spend every waking hour sharpening my Scrabble skills; I would get so good that I'd walk in there in my underwear and beat her by four hundred points.

I slept badly and showed up at the office the following day in a foul mood. It didn't help when Myrna told me that Harvey wanted to see me. Seeing Harvey was never a good thing. I had never walked out of Harvey's office feeling better than when I had walked in.

"Sit down," he said, ushering me in. "You look like shit."

"I didn't sleep well last night."

"You should sleep. Sleep is important. You can't do this type of work without sleeping."

---

[67]As is *cocksucker*, *cocktease* is not hyphenated when used as a noun.

Harvey leaned back in his old swivel chair, lit a Lucky Strike, and inhaled so deeply that I felt like coughing. He liked to affect the 1940s private eye look, the loosened tie, the shabby suit, the unfiltered cigarettes.

"Let me tell you what I'm thinking here, all right?"

I nodded blankly, knowing he would.

"I think it's time to expand our list."

"Expand our list?"

"Yeah. We're in a rut. We're doing the same old books every month—ditzy blonde with big tits from Nebraska moves into a new building and gets fucked nine ways from Sunday by everyone who lives there, bimbo from Oklahoma gets buttfucked by an entire bunkhouse of cowboys, airline stewardess goes down on the crew in the cockpit thirty-five thousand feet over the Grand Canyon, et cetera, et cetera. . . . You follow me?"

"More or less."

"We're basically servicing the same market, your basic meat whompers. And we're doing okay. We're a cash cow for this fucking house. Not that they would ever take a moment to acknowledge this fact. Would it kill them to say once in a while, 'Hey, guys, nice work. Thanks to you, we can publish all those dickheads who want to write the Great American Novel and sell eleven copies?'"

I was used to Harvey's disjointed ramblings. They went on for a while before getting to the point, so I merely sat there and nodded or shook my head appropriately as he went on.

"So I'm thinking, maybe there's another market out there. An untapped market. Maybe we could do dogs."

"Dogs?"

"Yeah, dogs. We could try horses also, but that gets a little too bizarro. I don't even think Linda Lovelace[68] could do a horse. You ever see a horse's dick?"

"Not really. . . . Harvey, what are you talking about?"

"Women and dogs."

"Women *and* dogs. You mean . . . *having sex with dogs?*"

"Yeah. It's a big sexual fantasy for a lot of women."

"How do you know?"

"I've heard. So what do you say? You want to write one?"

"A book about women having sex with dogs?"

"Yeah. I'll pay you a grand instead of eight hundred. Because it's a new genre, and you might want to do some research. You could find some women who are into it, ask them how they get the dog hard. Do they go down on him? Do they give him a hand job? What happens when the dog comes?"

"Harvey, forget it."

"What do you mean, forget it? How hard could it be? It's basically the same thing but you got a paw instead of a leg, and you don't light up a cigarette afterward."

"I'm not interested."

"Why not?"

"Because I don't know how dogs fuck!"[69]

* * *

I didn't hear from Karen IX for over a week. When she did call me the next time, she called me at home late on a Monday night.

---

[68]Glottistically talented actress, née Linda Boreman (1949–2002), whose 1969 debut film, *Dog Fucker,* aka *Linda and the German Shepherd,* led her to star in the seminal porno blockbuster *Deep Throat* in 1972.

[69]During his period in Hollywood, William Faulkner was put on a costumed period drama called *Land of the Pharaohs* by Warner Brothers. Faulkner went to his office conscientiously every day and stared blankly at his Underwood. After a fruitless week he went to tell Jack Warner he couldn't write the script because he "didn't know how pharaohs talked."

"I was expecting your call," she said in her sex kitten voice.

"Why would I do that?"

"To take another crack."

"And why would I be interested in *taking another crack?*"

"You could win."

"I don't think I could."

"What if I only wore only two articles of clothing?"

"That's not the point."

There was silence on the phone for a number of seconds. Then, "Ah, hell hath no fury like a man scorned. Is that it?"

"That's it."

"Don't you think playing a little hard to get is kind of stimulating?"

"You weren't the one standing at attention."

"It was a very impressive sight, believe me."

Oh, Jesus. It was happening again. The loss of all principle, the disintegration of all resolve in the face of a little ego stroking.

"All you have to do is score a hundred points."

"A hundred?" I heard myself saying.

"Uh-huh. I'll wear nothing but a bra and panties. On point one hundred and one, I'll be completely naked. What do you say?"

What did I say? I said, "How about tomorrow night?"

"I'm working this week. How about Friday?"

"Friday's good."

"Eight o'clock. I'll make dinner."

"Skip the dinner."

I had four days to get ready. I went into rigorous training. Early to bed, exercise, tuna fish three times a day. I bought a Scrabble dictionary and checked out abstruse little words. I stockpiled them: *zoa, adz, qat, xeme, keb*. . . . I clipped them on my belt like hand grenades.

When I walked in the door of her apartment at eight sharp on

Friday night, I was ready for combat. The place was candlelit. There was Chopin on the stereo. She was wearing a short bathrobe, heels, and earrings. Some exquisite perfume drifted into my brain. She was clearly trying to tilt the playing field.

"You're not taking any chances, are you?" I remarked.

"Home court advantage. A little Pouilly-Fumé?"

"Nope."

"You sure? It's very good."

"Let's do it."[70]

The Scrabble board was set up near the window, looking out over Lexington Avenue. Pouring herself a glass of wine, she brought over an ice bucket and placed it beside the board. Then she slipped out of her bathrobe, revealing a black lacy bra and, the ultimate weapon, a thong, right out of the Victoria's Secret catalog.

How does a man defend himself against a thong? Years later, we would learn that it was a thong that nearly brought down the government of the most powerful nation on earth.

I offered her the letter bag. She picked an *a*. I picked a *t*. Not an auspicious beginning. She nearly Scrabbled on the first word. I was down thirty-eight to zip before I had even gone. I stared at my rack. It was either that or stare at her.

Once again I had poor letters. It was bad enough that I had the thong to contend with. I had a rack full of vowels as well. It didn't take long to lose my tie, belt, and shirt. But I didn't care. What did I need clothes for?

Her bra went on my fourth turn when I hit a thirty-two-point double word score with *gledge*.[71] Frankly, I would have preferred she kept it on. It was a tactical disadvantage having to sit a few feet away from a pair of lovely candlelit breasts.

[70]Reportedly Gary Gilmore's last words before the Utah firing squad.
[71]A sly and cunning look.

Gradually, however, I began to close the gap. I got the *z* on a triple letter score with *zooid*[72] and got the thong off. But that, too, was beside the point, though she did her best to make it the point by adjusting her posture suggestively and resorting to a full Sharon Stone.[73]

To no avail. I remained focused on the board. I was able to stay in the game by an intense, almost Zen-like discipline. I was emitting an alternative radio frequency in order to jam her signals. There was a beautiful naked woman sitting on the couch sipping Pouilly-Fumé, and I was in another world, making up words, sorting letters in my rack maniacally.

Maybe it was all that tuna fish. Maybe it was her resorting to overkill. Whatever it was, it was working. I was unnerving her. She hated the fact that I could tune her out at will. And to make matters worse, even though I was as naked as she was, I was not saluting her. The radio signal jamming was working. She was not getting the tribute she felt she deserved, and it infuriated her.

And as her fury increased, her Scrabble skills diminished just enough to give me a shot. Between her loss of composure and a windfall of good letters, I pulled ahead briefly, then fell behind, then pulled ahead again.

There were only seven points separating us when we started to play out. She was bent over the board, concentrating furiously, her breasts swaying indifferently in front of her. She looked like a mad-woman in a nineteenth-century insane asylum. I kept that image in my head all the way to the end.

I played out with *obex*[74] and sat back and breathed an enormous

---

[72]An independent organism produced by other than sexual methods.

[73]Movie star and former Miss Pennsylvania, whose career was launched by the riveting snatch shot in the 1992 hit *Basic Instinct*.

[74]An obstacle or preventative.

sigh, perhaps not of triumph exactly but of something between exhaustion and intoxication.

I felt as good as I could remember feeling in a long while. Chopin was still coughing up blood over the piano keys, but I was impervious to him, and to the perfume, and to her.

"Congratulations," she said, without meaning it.

I looked at her sitting across the battlefield from me. She had never looked better. And less desirable. All my testosterone had been spent in the conquest. I had won the battle. And lost the war.

At that moment, I knew that all I would have to do to get my revenge would be to put my clothes on and walk out the door. It would kill her, after the perfume and the thong, to have a man walk out on her.

Believe me, I thought about it. After what she had put me through, the humiliation, the tuna fish, she deserved it. But I couldn't do it. I wish I could say that it was entirely compassion, but I would be lying.

There is a time and place for compassion, and this wasn't it.

Karen IX was not a mercy fuck. Not by any stretch of the imagination. So I got up, poured myself a glass of wine, went over to her tape deck, and found a Chet Baker cassette.

I took her hand, and we started to dance in the candlelight, high above Lexington Avenue. Chet barely got through "My Funny Valentine" before we were on the floor, going at it on the deep-pile rug, just like Audrey and the air-conditioning repairman.

To this day I consider the Chet Baker, Pouilly-Fumé post-Scrabble dance on the floor with Karen IX to be in the top ten.

I walked out of there that night feeling as good as I was going to feel with a woman like that. Any woman who takes showers for construction workers and resorts to a thong to win a Scrabble game isn't what you're looking for in life.

To tell you the truth, I don't think she really liked men all that much. There wasn't a lot of tenderness in her. It was all about performance with her. Either you scored four hundred or you didn't.

* * *

As it turned out, my instincts about her were dead on. Ten years or so afterward, I was in Las Vegas on a gambling junket. Late one night, as I was leaving the craps tables at the Mirage after a very bad run, I decided to stop at the bar to drown my sorrows.

At first I thought it was a hallucination. Karen IX was sitting alone at the end of the bar in a faux mink stole, a half-drunk whiskey sour in front of her, a cigarette burning indifferently in her hand. It was the complete picture. If Cézanne had wandered in he would have painted her.

I stood in the doorway, thinking of what I could say to her. I tried to come up with the appropriate line, but for the life of me, I couldn't think of a word. Not a single word. I had all the letters but couldn't make a word out of them.

So I turned around and walked out. The faint scent of her perfume floated on the desert air. The taste of Pouilly-Fumé rose in my throat. Chet Baker crept up on the soundtrack. And as I disappeared into the rarefied neon heat of the Las Vegas night, I wondered what her price was.

X

THE KINDNESS OF NEIGHBORS

I arrived in Los Angeles in January 1981, the first month of the first year of the first Reagan administration. I remember watching the inauguration in a bar on Sepulveda Boulevard, drinking Budweiser and eating pretzels. The TV sound was off, and Tammy Wynette was singing "Stand by Your Man" on the jukebox. Nobody in the bar was talking. People just stared up at the screen, blinking sporadically.

Two days before I arrived, there had been an earthquake in Palmdale that hit 5.2 on the Richter. I had felt my first aftershock stopping for gas in San Bernardino. I was seriously considering turning right around and heading back into the sunrise. But I had only about a millimeter left on my clutch and would have never made it.

Only a few weeks before, Vanessa Vellacruz had written her last title, *Swamp Hoyden*,[75] picked up her check, packed her 1969 VW Beetle, and headed for the Holland Tunnel. I had a little less than two grand in my pocket and a vague idea of making my fortune as a screenwriter in Hollywood.

Like a lot of refugees from the East, I was going to California to reach the edge of the continent, so I simply drove west until I hit the ocean and started looking for a place to live. I wound up in an off-peach stucco apartment building on Horizon Avenue in Venice, a

[75]Published in Great Britain under the title *Fallen Woman of the Marshes*.

block and a half from the ocean: $245 a month, including utilities. There was some old furniture that the previous tenant had left, including a TV set that got only one channel and then poorly and only at night. From my bathroom window, if you stood on the toilet seat, you could see the Pacific. You could smell it and hear it all the time.

The walls of 79 Horizon Avenue were so thin you could practically hear your neighbors thinking. The building seemed to be inhabited by characters out of a John Fante[76] novel. They moved around at odd hours, listened to odd music, cooked odd things on their illegal hot plates. There was a pervasive aroma of Parmesan cheese and marijuana. That, and the sound of unanswered telephones. It appeared as if no one was ever home, or if they were, they weren't interested in talking to anyone.

I spent my days working on a screenplay about my life as a cabdriver in New York—a sort of *Taxi Driver* with a happier ending. It was called *The West Side Highway,*[77] and when I finished it, I planned to sell it to Warner Bros. for $400,000, buy a Porsche, and move to Malibu.

It was a lonely time. I walked on the deserted beach thinking dark, winterish thoughts and wondering why I had left New York. The bars I hung out in at night were stark, unsociable places. People drank and watched television.

In February the rains came. It poured like hell for days on end. Rivulets ran through the streets. Garbage washed up on the beach. There was a Kafkaesque water stain on the ceiling of my apartment that kept getting bigger.

---

[76]Cult L.A. novelist (1909–1983), author of *Dago Red, The Brotherhood of the Grape,* and *Wait Until Spring, Bandini,* the last made into a film in 1989 starring Joe Mantegna and Faye Dunaway, which is not mentioned on either actor's résumé.

[77]Registered, Writers Guild of America.

It was at this point, the point at which I was calculating how much money I would need to fix my clutch, put gas in the car, drive three thousand miles, and have enough money left over to pay the first and last month on an apartment in Manhattan, that I met Karen Kraft.

Karen Kraft was her stage name. Her real name was Karen Mahalia. She had figured no one would go see a movie starring Karen Mahalia and changed it upon her arrival in L.A. from Bogalusa, Louisiana.

Actually, I heard Karen Kraft before I saw her. One day as I was slogging through a particularly rough patch of my script, I heard the unmistakable prose of Tennessee Williams floating through the thin walls of my apartment.

" . . . *it's wonderfully fitting that Belle Reve should finally be these bunch of old papers in your capable hands . . .*"

I waited for Stanley Kowalski to answer, to tell her about how this here state of Louisiana had the Napoleonic Code, but he said nothing.

" . . . *Oh, I suppose he's just not the type who goes for Jasmine perfume . . .*"

It went on for some time, Blanche DuBois going slowly off the deep end in that sweltering apartment in New Orleans. The voice was authentically southern, and though it may not have been Vivien Leigh, it wasn't chopped liver either. I was moved by the fragility, the nostalgia, the world-weariness in that voice.

For the next few mornings, always it seemed at just the time I started working, Blanche DuBois wafted through my wall. I was thinking of knocking on her door and asking her if she could keep it down a little when she knocked on my door. It was late afternoon, the sun sinking heavily into the Pacific, and I was nodding out on my couch after another barren day at the typewriter.

I stumbled to the door, opened it, and barked, "What?"

She looked at me with moist eyes. She had the ability, I would learn, to create drama out of the most banal of exchanges.

"Terribly sorry to have disturbed you," she said in her lilting Blanche DuBois voice. "Karen Kraft. Your neighbor. Pleasure to meet you."

We shook hands. It seemed a strangely cold gesture, after all that overheated Tennessee Williams.

"I wonder if I could impose upon you for a small favor," she said, as I kept my eyes on hers. We were standing so close together that it was difficult for me to get a good look at her.

"Sure."

"I have an audition."

"You're an actress?"

"Yes. I hope I have not been disturbing you. I'm doing a scene study class with Yves Turner, and I chose *Streetcar,* and well, you know, what happens with Tennessee—"

"Don't worry. I don't even hear it."

"I was wondering if I left my door open, could you answer my phone?"

"No problem."

"If you'd just say, 'Karen Kraft's line,' I'd be much obliged."

"Sure."

"I intend to get a service as soon as the check from my last job arrives."

We stood in my doorway, caught up in the vacuum of the moment. Then she said, "Well, I don't know how to thank you." And she gave me a smile and headed down the hall toward the elevator.

I watched her retreat, getting my first real look at her. She was maybe five two, on the thin side, with frizzy brunette hair and nice legs. She was wearing some sort of sarong-type skirt, an old shawl, and a pair of rickety heels. Arriving at the elevator, she pressed the down button, turned and waved. I waved back.

The phone did not ring that afternoon, but I did not desert my post. I was heating up a can of chicken gumbo soup on my illegal hot plate when I heard her heels clicking down the hall. She appeared in my open doorway and looked at me hopefully.

"I'm afraid nobody's called," I told her.

"Thanks ever so much," she said and she swept off, incipient tears gathering in her eyes.

* * *

This routine went on for a while. Whenever she had an audition she would ask me to answer her phone, which never rang. One afternoon, curiosity got the better of me, and after she left I went next door to have a look around. I justified this invasion of privacy by convincing myself that it was the job of a writer to delve into the recesses of the human soul.

Her apartment was cluttered with oddly matched furniture, magazines, a collection of antique dolls, and a lot of old clothes. I poked through her wardrobe of period costumes, checked out her medicine cabinet full of cosmetics and over-the-counter painkillers. On her desk were a number of scripts for TV shows, poetry books, and plays. Besides Williams, there was a lot of Eugene O'Neill.

From the look of things, this was not a happy woman.

The phone rang. I picked up.

"Karen Kraft's line," I said, attempting to sound like a professional answering service operator.

"Oh, hi. It's me. You sound very good, like a real answering service."

I didn't know whether this was a compliment or not.

"Were there any calls?"

"I'm afraid not."

"You know what they say, the real answering service operators, when there are no calls? They say, 'You're all clear.'"

"Got it."

"Honey. 'You're all clear, *honey*.' May I impose upon you for another little favor?"

"Of course."

"If Jason calls, could you tell him that I can't rehearse tomorrow afternoon because I have another audition, but perhaps we can get together tomorrow night."

"Okay."

"Much obliged."

Jason called an hour later. I got the phone on the fourth ring.

"Karen Kraft's line," I said a little breathlessly.

"Shit."

Though he had uttered only one syllable, I knew immediately that it was Stanley Kowalski on the other end of the line.

"She was supposed to be there."

"Is this Jason?"

"Yeah."

"She left a message for you."

I repeated the message.

He said *shit* again, then said, "Tell her I can't do tomorrow night. Ask her about Thursday morning."

He hung up without saying thank you.

* * *

It was after midnight when she got home, if she did in fact get home that night. I know this because I had waited up till midnight to give her the message, then went to sleep. At about ten o'clock the following morning I went next door and knocked.

She came to the door, opened it a crack, and peeked out. She looked as if she hadn't slept. Her eye makeup was smudged. I could smell wine on her breath.

"How're you doing?" I asked, though it was clear from one look at her that she wasn't doing well.

"Oh . . . hello . . ." She squinted at me as if I were some distant relative whom she only vaguely remembered.

"Just wanted to give you your messages."

"My messages?"

"Actually, there was only one. From Jason. He said he needs to know about Thursday."

"Thursday?"

"You told me to tell him yesterday that you couldn't rehearse tomorrow, which would be today, but then he called and suggested Thursday morning yesterday, which would be today, and, you weren't here or, it seems, there, because he called again earlier this morning to ask where you were."

This was all a little too complex to assimilate in her present state of mind. She closed her eyes, reopened them, and said, "I'm terribly sorry to have put you to all this trouble."

"It's all right. Just being a good neighbor."

"Well, I have always depended upon the kindness of neighbors."

And suddenly she was back into character. I smiled, and she smiled back. But it wasn't the smile of someone enjoying a witty exchange; it was the lacquered boozy smile of southern women who drank.

"May I offer you a cup of coffee?"

And then, without waiting for my answer, she said, "Would you be kind enough to give me a few minutes to freshen up?"

When I entered her apartment ten minutes later I saw that she had done a little more than just freshen up. She had put her hair up, dabbed a little perfume somewhere, and changed into a black sweater and jeans. The blackness of the sweater accentuated the whiteness of her skin. Her eyes reflected that opaque sorrow that made you think she had personally lived through all the tragedies she played as an actress.

In the less forgiving mid-morning light, it was clear that she was older than I had thought, closer to forty than to thirty. Life did not appear to have been kind to her. Her face was a road map of tribulation. There was, nonetheless, a fragile classic beauty to her, a pentimento that emerged through the hardness and was made more striking by it.

She poured the coffee with a reasonably steady hand, in spite of the fact that she was badly hungover. Her innate politeness carried her over the rough spots. With that ingrained grace that southern women have, she asked me about myself.

I wound up telling her more than I had planned on. She was easy to talk to. I told her about my taxi driver and how his stoic nihilism was slowly being penetrated by the love of a good woman.

At some point during the synopsis of my screenplay, she stopped listening. Her eyes went dead on me, and though she was still looking at me, there was nobody home. She was tuned to a different station.

When I stopped talking, she continued to look at me blankly for a moment, then said, very earnestly, "If you think you can get away with that, you got something else coming to you."

"Excuse me?"

"You think you own this whole town, don't you? Well let me tell *you* something, Mr. J. R. Ewing[78]—we're not leaving Dallas, not today, not tomorrow, not ever . . . not—"

---

[78]Lead character, played by Larry Hagman, of the wildly successful nighttime TV soap opera *Dallas* (1978–1991), in which oil-rich Texans did despicable things to one another.

She stopped, lowered her eyes, shook her head. "Not . . ." She was spinning her wheels, trying to find the next word.

Then, abruptly, she turned back to me and said, "Some more coffee?"

The transition was seamless. We were no longer in J. R. Ewing's office in Dallas but back in Venice, California, drinking coffee in her apartment.

"Well, I'm afraid I've taken too much of your time," she said, getting up. I wasn't sure whether she was speaking to me or to Larry Hagman. "I'm sure you've got work to do on your screenplay."

"Yes . . . ," I said, taking the cue. "Thanks for the coffee."

"It was my pleasure, I assure you," she said, reverting to her mannered southern politeness.

When I got back to my apartment I splashed some cold water on my face and thought about what had just happened. Was it one of those techniques they taught in acting class? Was it a little joke I didn't pick up on? Or was she out of her mind?

A few days later she showed up at my door around ten o'clock at night in a white coat that had ASSISTANT MEDICAL EXAMINER stitched on it.

"I know it's late," she said, "but I wonder if I could impose upon you for just a very few minutes of your time. I have an audition tomorrow morning for *Quincy*, and I would be very grateful if you could run the lines with me. It won't take but a moment."

I invited her in. The place was a mess, as usual. But she didn't seem to notice anything. She handed me the script and said, "You can start with the line about traces of cyanide in the dog food." She began to pace back and forth across my apartment.

I found my line and read it. "I'm seeing twenty-five cc's of cyanide in the kibble. I bet you she put the rest in Mr. Weston's omelette."

"But why kill the dog too?"

"To make it look like the cook went mad and cover her traces."

"You really think so?"

"You bet, doll," I said, giving the line a little Jack Klugman inflection.

"What are you going to do?"

"Call Homicide."

"The poor dog . . ." She got a little weepy reading this line.

"The poor husband," I said, turned the page, and discovered that there was nothing else. The scene was over. Klugman had the button line.

She broke character and looked at me quizzically. "I wonder if I should cry really loud on the line about the dog. She's a new assistant he just hired. She's studying forensic medicine. She probably has a little crush on him—what do you think? I mean, she's had a hard life, maybe comes from a broken home, alcoholic father, that type of thing. The dog means a lot to her. He reminds her of a dog she used to have when she was a little girl . . ."

She told me about a beagle named Bubba she'd had when she was a girl that had gotten run over by a melon truck. The dog's spirit visited her now and then. She knew he was somewhere looking over her, possibly in Mar Vista.

Her pale hands moved as she spoke. When she tried to keep them still, they trembled. She needed a drink.

The pain of watching her struggle got to me. I offered her a beer, and she looked at me as if I were Saint Jude.

The beer stilled her hands, and she told me more about her life. She left Bogalusa when she was seven, moved to Mobile, was president of her drama club in high school. Did some local TV, then went to New York, worked on a soap, came out to L.A. in the mid-seventies, did some waiver theater, a guest role on *The Wal-tons . . .*"[79]

And then, while we were on our second beer, it happened again. Suddenly, in the middle of a description of a performance she did of *Summer and Smoke,* she said, "I really need this job, Mr. Carrington.[80] Philip left me without a penny, just up and abandoned me with two children and his gambling debts . . ."

Her eyes were straight ahead, focused on the window behind me, as if John Forsythe were standing there in his tuxedo.

"I'll tell you everything she does, I promise. You'll know every move Alexis Colby[81] makes before she even makes it . . ."

There was nothing to do but sit there and wait for the scene to play out. It didn't take very long. A half dozen lines and it was over. And as soon as it was over, she was back in my easy chair drinking beer, as if we hadn't just taken a little detour into the twisted world of *Dynasty.*

I didn't say anything, afraid that asking her about it directly would be like waking a sleepwalker while she was sleepwalking.

"It's late. I should be going," she said abruptly. She got up from the chair and handed me the empty beer can. "Thanks ever so much," she said and was gone.

*　*　*

The next morning she peeked in and asked me to answer her phone again when she went to her *Quincy* audition. I didn't know how to say no.

---

[79]1970s TV show about a large Depression-era West Virginia family who wore overalls and had frequent heart-to-heart talks.

[80]Character, played by John Forsythe, in the wildly successful prime-time TV series *Dynasty,* about a bunch of filthy rich people in Denver who did despicable things to one another.

[81]*Dynasty* character, played by Joan Collins, the ageless British actress for whom the author wrote the 1986 CBS miniseries *Monte Carlo,* in which she sang "The Last Time I Saw Paris," was captured by the Nazis for spying, and spent thirty-five pages in a Gestapo prison without a single wardrobe change.

It rang about 11:00 A.M. It was Stanley Kowalski. I told him she was auditioning for *Quincy*.

"Did she leave a message?"

"No."

"Shit."

"Stanley, can I talk to you?"

"What do you mean, can I talk to you? And why are you calling me *Stanley*?"

"I'm not an answering service operator." I leveled with him. "I'm her next-door neighbor. I answer her phone as a favor. Look, I'm a little worried about her. And I don't want to talk about this on the phone. The walls are paper thin here. Could you meet me for a cup of coffee?"

He agreed to meet me at a coffee shop on Westminster and Ocean Front. As soon as he walked in the door I knew it was Stanley Kowalski. Besides the leather jacket, he had the hunched shoulders and the high-energy Brando fidgeting.

He sat down in the booth opposite me and ordered coffee while I told him about the peculiar episodes I had witnessed.

"That's weird, man," he said.

"How well do you know her?"

"She's in my acting class. We're doing *Streetcar* together. I figured she was a little out there but nothing like that."

He stirred his coffee pensively and then said, very seriously, "Maybe she's just doing Blanche."

"What do you mean, just doing Blanche?"

"Blanche goes crazy, remember? They got to bring the nurse and the doctor in at the end. So maybe Karen's just getting into character."

"But she's doing dialogue from TV shows—from *Dallas* and *Dynasty*. In the middle of talking about something else, she's suddenly having this conversation with Larry Hagman."

"She know Larry?"

"I don't know."

"I've been trying to get an audition for that show for months. I can do Texas, you know. I did a scene from *Giant* in class. You know the Jimmy Dean scene when the oil squirts up in his face?"

I searched his face for a trace of irony. But there was nothing there but James Dean grafted on top of Marlon Brando.

"You don't happen to know who the casting director is on *Dallas,* do you?"

I shook my head.

"Maybe I can get in there. That's a good show. And if they like your work they can write you in as a continuing character . . ."

I gave him my number and told him to call me if she started acting strangely, and, pleading an appointment, excused myself. Back in the apartment, I made an attempt to do some work but wound up just sitting and staring at the typewriter. I couldn't get her out of my mind.

She was one more wounded soul washed up on the beach of Southern California. The town was full of them—myself included. Maybe I didn't wear an assistant medical examiner's coat to rehearse for a scene about a coroner, maybe I didn't recite audition scenes for roles I wasn't going to get in television soap operas—but I had my own delusional world. I was flying below the radar too.

We were both refugees from somewhere else, living in our John Fante building, waiting to catch a wave. No one was calling either of us. We were both all clear.

* * *

And so I continued to answer her phone, which didn't ring. And to drink beer with her at night and witness the flights into her fantasy world. When she knocked on my door, I never knew who was going to be there. She would be Yvonne De Carlo, a schoolmarm from *The Waltons,* a hooker from *Hill Street Blues,* a corrupt lawyer trying to swindle the Carringtons on *Dynasty,* and, inevitably, Rita Hayworth.

The night she came to my door as Rita was in early April. The windows were open, and there was a ripeness coming from the ocean. She had put on a forties dress that was ripped at the shoulder and overdone the makeup.

She had a bottle of tequila with her. We didn't bother with the salt or lemons. I dimmed the lights and we played a scene out of one of her movies. It was either *The Lady from Shanghai* or *Salome,* I wasn't sure. And I was either Orson Welles or Stewart Granger. Not that it made a lot of difference because I didn't know my lines.

I found a jazz station on the radio, and we drank and danced and got loaded. Inevitably, we wound up rolling around on my bed before passing out. It was like two drowning swimmers pulling each other under. It was either our finest or our worst moment.

When I woke at dawn she was gone. I lay there in the foggy early morning waiting for the tequila hangover, the world's worst hangover, to kick in. When it did, it was at least a 6.5 on the Richter. I buried my head under the pillow to wait it out.

In the middle of the hangover the phone rang. My phone. I picked it up in order to stop the ringing, which was splitting my head down the middle like a machete through a ripe cantaloupe. It was Stanley Kowalski.

"Hey, man, I been calling her all morning. You're not answering her phone no more?"

"I'm not feeling very well . . ."

"Listen, could you tell her I got a job? Recurring role on *The Incredible Hulk.* I play a union organizer with cerebral palsy. I get to work in a wheelchair. Isn't that great?"

"Terrific."

I hung up, went next door and knocked. There was no answer. I tried the door and found it, as usual, unlocked. She wasn't there. The bed was made. The windows closed. The phone was on the hook.

Unable to go back to sleep, I went for a walk on the beach. It was one of those hazy April days when the sun doesn't burn through the cloud cover until the middle of the afternoon. The beach was empty except for an occasional jogger or stray dog. It was so foggy that you could barely see the buildings along Ocean Front Walk.

I trudged north toward Santa Monica, hands buried in my pockets, deep in murky thought. It wasn't clear to me whether I was looking for her or trying to escape from her. As it happened, I nearly bumped into her.

She emerged out of the fog like a vision, walking barefoot along the surf line, still in her Rita Hayworth outfit. She was walking right toward me, backlit by the late morning sun.

She walked right past me. I went after her, calling her name. When she didn't answer I caught up and took her hand.

"Karen," I said quietly.

"One day out on the ocean I will die—with my hand in the hand of a nice-looking ship's doctor."

I took her hand, and we walked silently back through the fog to her apartment. I put her to bed, lowered the shades, waited till she was asleep, and returned to my apartment.

Hours went by. I sat in my chair, not knowing what to do. I wasn't a relative, or really even a close friend. I was a drinking companion. I ran lines with her, both real and fictional. I answered her phone.

It was late afternoon, the sun sinking quickly, and I had dozed off in my chair when I heard a knock at her door. I got up and went out into the hall and found Sergeant Glotz, the landlord, outside her apartment. He was a big unpleasant man with a scary look in his eye and a nasty Robitussin habit. He had been hit by a Viet Cong shell in Pleiku and had a metal plate in his head.

"You know where she is?" he said.

"She's not feeling well."

"Well, when you see her tell her she's out of here Monday if she don't pay the rent."

"She hasn't paid the rent?"

"Not since January. Less she wants to suck my dick every night for a month, she's on the street Monday morning at 0700."

I waited for him to go back downstairs, then went next door. You could see very little through the drawn shades. I sat down on the bed beside her and watched over her until she opened her eyes.

I could tell from her look of panic that she had no idea who I was or, for that matter, who she was. Trembling, she held on to me, then leaned back on the pillow. After a long moment, she smiled and said, *"The three of us drove out to Moon Lake Casino, very drunk and laughing all the way."*

She was stuck in Blanche DuBois mode. I sat in her chair for hours as she recited disjointed lines from the play in no particular order.

I stayed with her all night long, dozing fitfully in the chair, waiting for morning. I had decided not to call at night. It would go more easily in the morning.

A little after seven I made the phone call. The ambulance was there in under an hour. There was a man and a woman, just like in *Streetcar.* They were gentle with her. And she, of course, was superb. She knew exactly how to play this scene.

"I have always depended on the kindness of strangers," she purred in that perfect tragic voice, filled equally with hope and despair.

I called the hospital that night and was told that she was resting comfortably. When I asked if I could visit, I was told not for a while.

* * *

That while stretched into a month. I called every few days to check up on her but was told she wasn't ready to have visitors. April drifted into May, and with it my thoughts of her began to recede into the foggy memory of winter.

A new neighbor moved in, a nocturnal person whom I never saw but whose pacing kept me awake at night. Sergeant Glotz had her furniture hauled away by Goodwill. I kept some of her books and a suitcase full of her clothes.

Like Stanley, I finally got lucky. I was hired to write an episode of *B.J. and the Bear.* It was about the two twin truck drivers in cutoff jeans, Teri and Geri, entering the Miss California contest. Drawing on my experience at Midworld Books, I threw in a hot tub scene. They loved it.

In July, I got a phone call from her doctor at the hospital and was told I could visit her. I drove out to a hospital in the Valley.

As I sat waiting for her in the visitors' room, a cheerful, sun-drenched alcove that reeked of ammonia, I wondered who she was going to be.

When I saw her walking down the hall with an intern, I barely recognized her. She was wearing a sweater and skirt that looked like it came from Montgomery Ward. Her hair was washed and combed and cut short. She had white tennis shoes on.

She sat down opposite me and smiled. I could see the medication around the edges of the smile. Blanche was gone, as were Rita Hayworth, Joan Collins, and the rest of them. What was left was Karen

Mahalia, a girl from Bogalusa, Louisiana, who had come to Holly-wood to make it as an actress and skidded off the rails.

We talked fitfully, mostly about me. She retained that southern woman's ability to engage a man by letting him talk about himself. It was a painful half hour. There seemed to be very little left of my next-door neighbor. I wondered where she had gone. What had the medication done with her?

And then, as I was leaving, the Karen I knew came back for a moment. Just long enough to reassure me that there was a piece of her still inside. We had shaken hands, and she was about to accompany the intern back to the ward when she looked at me and asked, "Have I gotten any phone calls?"

It was a perfect line reading. She delivered it three-quarters profile to camera right, making sure that the key light would illuminate her face.

I hesitated for just a moment and then said, "You're all clear, honey."

XI

A LITTLE DEATH IN THE HÔTEL
DEBUSSY

I knew Karen Jones for less than two hours. And Jones, I'm sure, wasn't her real name. But I include her in this anthology of Karens because in many respects she was a typical Karen. And because she was the last Karen, as well as the only Karen I committed adultery with.

Though I did, in fact, have sexual relations with a woman while married to someone else, there were mitigating circumstances involved. At least it certainly felt that way at the time.

Up until then I had been relatively faithful to my first wife. I have to qualify the qualifying adverb *relatively* because I did stray twice in the course of that marriage. Twice was a number, according to a French friend of mine, that would qualify me, in France at least, for sainthood.

We were sitting, my French friend and I, in a brasserie near the Place St. Sulpice in Paris, enjoying a very good lunch and a couple of bottles of an excellent Loire Valley red wine. Seventy-five milliliters of Chinon at noon tends to loosen you up, and Philippe and I had gotten around to the inevitable subject of women. He was in a moribund marriage, or what's called in France a *mariage d'immobilier* or real estate marriage. He and his wife co-owned an exquisite apartment off the Luxembourg Gardens that was worth so much money that neither of them could afford to buy out the other's equity. And so they reached a tacit but nonetheless elaborately constructed accommodation that enabled them to cheat on each other systematically while remaining under the same roof.

When I asked him how this arrangement worked, he replied that the secret was not asking questions. What you don't know can't hurt you, *n'est-ce pas?*

When he asked me how I dealt with the constrictions of my marriage, I confessed that I dealt with them badly. Once, a few years ago, after too much tarragon in my trout at lunch, I had wound up on the floor of my office with a temp secretary in a very short skirt; and a couple of months after that incident, a friend's wife and I had consummated a number of years of random flirting with a wrestling match in the back of her Subaru.

"*Ça,*" he said, his eyes glowing from the Chinon, "*c'est presque la sainteté.*" It would be the first, and last, time in my life I would be accused of sainthood.

I cite these facts as preamble to establish a frame of reference for my hour and forty-five minutes with Karen Jones. I was married and very unhappy. And so, presumably, was my wife at the time, this non-Karen I had married a number of years ago and gradually fallen out of love with. It wasn't so much our real estate that was keeping us together as it was our inertia. Neither of us wanted to fire the first shot. But the idea of ending the marriage had been present in my mind and undoubtedly in hers for a while before my fateful trip to Paris.

So it happened that when I met Karen Jones I had already spoken to a lawyer friend, who had explained to me a number of unpleasant facts about California family law at the time. "You're basically fucked, one way or the other," he said. "You walk out, you might as well just go straight to the cleaners." This dire prediction may have had a bearing on what was to follow.

As cute-meets go, this was about as cute as they get. It was late September in Paris. We were each backing away from one of Monet's water lilies hung on either side of the little rotunda downstairs at the Marmottan Museum, in the Sixteenth Arrondissement, when we literally backed into each other.

The very first impression I had of this woman, whom I had not yet seen, was promising. I could feel the panty elastic through the fabric of her dress, as well as smell the faint fragrance of expensive perfume. I processed this in that remote area of the brain where men process this type of information before turning around.

We said *"excusez-moi"* simultaneously and both immediately knew from the accent that neither of us was French. Then we looked at each other. They were frank, searching looks, more than embarrassed glances. Then we both laughed. Then she spoke. "Monet looks better from a distance."

The voice was standard American but without that nasal flatness that characterizes midwestern speech. She was on the tall side, maybe five seven, with long blond hair tied behind her back. Her skin was fair, lightly freckled, and she had off-blue eyes and an interesting mouth. It was an eclectic mixture of features. Iowa mixed with Finland and maybe a touch of Poland.

It is always at this moment, when another sentence is required to keep the cute-meet going, that you wish you had some 1940s screenwriter composing lighthearted banter for you. There was a perfect line for this situation somewhere, but I didn't know it. There was a small flame flickering in a breeze that could go out any moment and, desperate to keep it going, I uttered the first thing that came into my mind.

"Do you come here often?"

Jesus, what a clunker. Of all the lines available in this situation, I had come up with a trite and completely inappropriate one.

I could see the beginnings of a frown on her lips and quickly added, "Of course, you don't come here often. You probably don't even live here."

"I'm visiting," she said.

"From where?"

"New York."

"Nice place to visit."

A microsmile.

"Can I ask you a question?"

I was tap dancing.

"Sure."

"You see that painting over there, the one with all the blue and green in it? Would you hang that in your living room?"

She looked at the painting, then back at me to see if I was being facetious, then shook her head.

"Me neither. It just looks like pond scum to me."

"Pond scum" made her laugh. And with that laugh I began to envisage the remainder of the day, if not the night. I was way ahead of myself. We hadn't even exchanged names yet, and I was already in bed with her.

With my lawyer's recent sobering words in mind, I began to formulate a game plan. I had the time and the opportunity and, I'm convinced, the motivation.

I was in Paris alone on business, with a free afternoon before flying back the next day to New York. It had been a disappointing trip. The business had been time-consuming and inconclusive; the weather had been gray and drizzly; I'd had two long, painful phone conversations with my future ex-wife, in which we tried to talk things over. Having this conversation over the telephone from different continents somehow freed us up, and we said things to each other that we had never said before and that, once said, could never be unsaid.

When I hung up, it was clear to me the marriage was terminal. At this point the only thing to do in order to put it out of its misery was to take it outside and shoot it. And I could think of no better way of accomplishing this than getting into trouble on my last day away from my wife.

To paraphrase my lawyer, if you're going to do the time, you might as well do the crime.

And so I checked the woman's left hand for a wedding ring. As if that mattered. There was none. I hadn't worn one in years—since I had accidentally (?) washed it down the drain in the men's room of Chicago's O'Hare Airport between flights.

We stood there, the seconds dissolving in front of us, our future slowly receding into the past.

"Have you been to Giverny?"[82] I asked her, while my mind careened through various considerations and calculations.

"No."

"It's very nice there. You can see the pond scum firsthand."

Another microsmile.

We were dying. It was time to take the plunge. I nonchalantly consulted my watch and went for it. "Have you had lunch?"

"No."

"Would you care to join me?"

---

[82]Tourist trap outside Paris where Claude Monet (1840–1926) retired in 1883 and compulsively painted his garden.

*   *   *

The Marmottan Museum is located in a residential neighborhood near the Bois de Boulogne. There are no restaurants in the immediate vicinity, as we soon discovered walking along the edge of the Jardins du Ranelagh, the little park that borders the museum.

A fine rain was falling, and neither of us had an umbrella. She was wearing a light raincoat and expensive shoes. I looked for a cab, but there weren't any.

When the rain increased we moved under a tree at the edge of the park. It was a big chestnut, richly green in the early afternoon light. It was the melancholy, diffused light of Indian summer, what the French call *l'arrière-saison*—the back season.

Standing under that tree, looking out across the park at a landscape more evocative of Manet than Monet, I felt as if we were in the middle of a painting, two figures in a sea of wet green. It was *Le Déjeuner sur l'Herbe*,[83] but she was wearing her clothes and we weren't eating. We were looking for a restaurant. Actually, we were looking for a hotel, but we didn't know it yet. At least not consciously.

Her raincoat was unbuttoned, and I could see the impression of her nipples against the thin fabric of her summer dress. This vision led to more unrestaurantlike thoughts. And it must have been why I noticed the hotel sign at that particular moment.

I saw it in the distance in a side street across the avenue from us. It was so small you had to be looking for it. I squinted through the rain, barely able to make it out. L'Hôtel Debussy.[84]

---

[83]Famous painting by the French artist Edouard Manet (1832–1883) in which a naked woman has lunch on the grass with two fully dressed men.

[84]Claude Debussy, French composer (1862–1918) of *La Mer* or, more familiarly, "Somewhere beyond the sea, somewhere . . . ," words originally written in French in 1936 by Charles Trenet on a train from Paris to Rouen on toilet paper, translated into English by Jack Lawrence in 1946, and recorded memorably by Bobby Darin in 1960.

"*Prélude à l'après-midi d'un faune*"[85] began to drift evocatively through my mind.

Her back was to the hotel, and, moreover, she may not have been thinking ahead in quite the same linear, purposeful fashion I was. But she wasn't necessarily thinking merely of lunch either because she looked at me and said exactly what I had been thinking. "I feel like we're in a painting."

"Which painting?" I asked.

"Our own painting."

"Do you like Debussy?"

"He was a musician, not a painter."

"I know. But I was just looking at a sign down that side street that says the Hôtel Debussy."

Consciously or not, I was planting the word *hotel* in her mind. And she responded accordingly. "Do you think they have a restaurant?"

"I doubt it."

We were down to subtext now, and I think she knew it as well as I did. The meaning was fragile and tenuous. It could have been so easily broken by the wrong words.

"What do you think you do at the Hôtel Debussy during the day in the rain?" I asked rhetorically.

"What they do at hotels during the day in the rain everywhere."

She turned around and looked across the street at the hotel sign in the distance, then turned back to me with a liquid look in her eyes.

I had already made my decision, but she was smarter than I was. She knew it could all be due to the filtered light of Paris on an af-

---

[85]Orchestral piece by the aforementioned composer, based on a poem by Mallarmé, in which a faun (Roman deity with goat's tail, pointed ears, and cloven feet) presumably contemplates having afternoon sex with a goddess.

ternoon in September, stimulated by all those water lilies and poppies and the ripe smell of the wet grass around us. She wanted a taste up front.

So she reached up and kissed me. It was a light kiss, a tasting kiss more than a passionate kiss. It was as if she were a wine buyer swirling the wine in the glass to appraise the nose before investing in it.

It didn't last very long, maybe five seconds. It wasn't even an hors d'oeuvre. More like a breadstick. But it did the trick.

We walked in silence across the Avenue Raphaël and up the side street to the hotel. I felt as if I was watching us through a long lens in a black-and-white French movie from the 1960s. Jean-Louis Trintignant and Anouk Aimée[86] approaching that dreary hotel in Normandy out of season as the rain fell and the Francis Lai score colored the soundtrack.

The Hôtel Debussy did not, unfortunately, belong in the movie. It was not old and charming but a renovated town house with a faux marble facade and an overly bright lobby with a mediocre bronze bust of the composer. And instead of there being a baggy-eyed room clerk in a faded cardigan with absinthe on his breath and a Gitane dripping from his mouth, there was a young North African in a Grateful Dead T-shirt chewing gum.

But they did have a room—Room 396 on the third floor. 675 francs. The room clerk did not bother to ask for passports or if there was luggage outside in the cab. This was France. This was two o'clock in the afternoon.

---

[86]Costars of the Claude Lelouch film in question, *A Man and a Woman,* in which Trintignant, racing his car in Monte Carlo, drives 800 kilometers in a driving rain to see Aimée in Paris, only to find that she's gone to Normandy; he then drives another 200 kilometers to Deauville, then runs another 100 meters across the deserted beach until he finds her and the camera does a 360-degree pan shot, while the famous *Da Da Da Dadadadada Da Da Da* score reaches a crescendo.

We rode up together in the rickety sardine-can elevator. It took a long time to climb a short distance, but we avoided eye contact. Our bodies, though, were millimeters apart. They couldn't have been any closer without touching.

Room 396 was at the end of hall, on the courtyard side. It didn't belong in the movie either. There was yellow wallpaper with birds, a bright blue carpet, a gold spread over a bed with polished wood headboard and uncomfortable bolster pillows. There was a badly antiqued armoire and a dressing table with a smudged mirror top and a cheap print of Montmartre over it.

I slipped the NE PAS DERANGER, S.V.P. sign over the doorknob and locked it behind me. She walked over to the window, parted the flimsy linen curtains, and looked out into the courtyard.

It would have been nice to have had a bottle of champagne in an ice bucket at this point. The room could have used some help. Yet with the gray light coming in from the window, backlighting her, I began to think that we could survive the room.

Tossing my jacket on the bed, I walked over, and without her turning around I slipped her raincoat off. I put my arms around her and pressed against her, looking out over the courtyard, small and sad in the rain. There was a cat curled up in the corner, and I thought of the Hemingway[87] story "Cat in the Rain," in which a woman tries to rescue a cat caught in the rain outside her hotel room in Italy as her indifferent husband lies on the bed reading.

Pulling her hair off her shoulders, I kissed the back of her neck. She took a deep breath but didn't turn around. My hands moved

---

[87]Ernest Hemingway (1899–1961) Nobel Prize–winning American writer of very short sentences, who ate his shotgun in Idaho in 1961.

over her. She breathed a little deeper. As I unbuttoned her dress, an entirely different movie began to appear in my mind's eye.

This movie had never been filmed before except in the remote recesses of my erotic fantasy life. This one was way out there where the buses didn't run. It involved making love to a woman whom I barely knew in a hotel room in a city I didn't live in. And it involved making love to her from the back without a word being uttered by either of us.

I slipped her dress down her body, nearly ripping it. She stepped out of it but kept her shoes on. I liked that. It was in my movie. Her bra and panties were both of flimsy black lace, and they hit the ground beside her shoes.

When she was naked except for her high heels and stockings, I moved back a few steps to admire her. I swore to myself that this was a moment I would never forget, whatever happened from here on in. I would take this to the grave with me. And I very well might. I kept it in mind, nurtured it, brought it back to life during those endless days in court listening to my wife's lawyer recite the litany of my sins. It nourished me and helped me make it through the aftermath of my afternoon at the Hôtel Debussy.

It was clear to me at that precise moment why painters painted. It was only the moment that counted—the frozen moment before it fell apart into component parts and the light changed and the music died away.

When I entered her she uttered a strangled cry. It was as if she were struggling for air. She must have had her own version of this faceless, wordless sexual fantasy because she came so quickly I thought she was crying. But I felt her eyes, and they were dry, and so I went on, and she came again, and I thought we both might die and go to Hell before it was over.

The French so aptly call an orgasm *la petite mort,* the little death. We both died a little, but she was lucky enough to die a little several times. Hera blinded Tiresias for telling the truth—that women enjoy sex more than men. And it was Karen Jones who made me understand the truth of that assertion there in that dreadful hotel room with the yellow wallpaper.

I carried her to the bed. Her eyes closed, she dozed on my shoulder as I listened to the rain and stared up at the low false ceiling that covered the beams.

When she opened her eyes again, the light had shifted. The afternoon had deepened. We looked at each other as if for the first time. In this new light, this subdued after-sex light, her makeup smudged, her hair damp with perspiration, she looked vulnerable to me, almost innocent.

We were suddenly shy with each other. After our tango at the window, it was hard to know how to reestablish contact.

"That was some lunch," I said, with a stab at 1940s screenwriter banter.

She nodded, creasing the corners of her mouth.

"This might be a good moment for introductions," I said.

I told her my name.

"Karen," she told me, and I managed not to laugh. "Karen Jones," she added, in a tone that clearly was an afterthought. We shook hands.

The shaking hands made us both laugh. But the laugh disintegrated, and we were left with the fact that we lying naked together on a hotel bed in the middle of the afternoon with perfect strangers.

She excused herself to go to the bathroom. Hearing her tinkle behind the thin door didn't help matters. When she reemerged, she realized that she was naked except for her stockings, and she grabbed her raincoat from the floor and put it on.

She lit a cigarette and sat back down on the bed.

"Now what?" I asked.

She shrugged.

"Lunch?" I suggested. We were going downhill fast.

She thought about that for a moment, then checked her watch.

"I have a meeting at four."

I looked at my watch. It was 2:45.

"You're here on business?" I asked.

"Yes. I'm a buyer for . . . Saks."

"That must be exciting."

"It's okay. How about you?"

I told her what I was there for.

I couldn't believe it. We were making small talk, as if we had just met in a bar. Instead of nibbling hors d'oeuvres, we had gone directly to dessert. And now neither of us had an appetite for lunch.

"So . . . ," I said. "Can I call you?"

"Okay. I'm at the . . . Crillon."

"Karen Jones?"

"Yes."

"If a man answers, should I hang up?"

"I'm here alone."

She kept her raincoat wrapped tightly around her as she gathered her clothes from the heap at the window and took them into the bathroom to change.

While she was getting re-dressed I got up and walked over to the window, peered out into the courtyard. The cat was gone. The rain was letting up. There was a window open across the way, and through it I could see a man sitting alone at his kitchen table reading a newspaper and eating a bowl of soup.

When she came out of the bathroom, she had touched up her makeup. We stood for a moment, not knowing what to say.

"I'll get you a cab."

"It's all right—there're a bunch of them in front of the museum."

"So . . . I'll call you then."

"Good."

Taking another glance at her watch, she said, "Sorry. Got to run."

"We'll have lunch," I said, trying one last shot at banter.

"Uh-huh," she said, letting the line lie on the floor.

I listened to the sound of her heels recede as she walked toward the elevator. I could hear the lumbering machine rising and the heavy door clanging shut. I didn't move for a while. I wanted to give her enough time to leave the building and find a taxi.

When I finally did leave, the room clerk gave me the obligatory *"Au revoir, monsieur."* I just nodded and avoided his eyes. I have no doubt that there was an amused expression on his face.

It was a long walk back from the Sixteenth Arrondissement to my hotel in St. Germain-de-Prés. But I was in no hurry. I walked slowly, crossing the river at the Trocadero and then heading east along the quay.

I felt as if the last two hours of my life had never happened. It was as if I had skipped lunch and gone to see a movie, and now I was back in the real world. There were unattractive people walking on the streets, buses, taxis, dog shit. There was no *Da Da Da Dadadadada Da Da Da* score in the background.

By the time I got to the Invalides I was starving. I found a bistro, ordered a *steak frites,* and devoured it. Then I sat back and watched Paris hurry by me, lost in a melancholy postcoital funk.

* * *

Frankly, I was not terribly surprised when I returned to my room, called the Crillon, and was told that there was no *Madame* or *Mademoiselle* Karen Jones at the hotel. I hoped that she had lied only about her last name.

My final night in Paris was uneventful. The thought of going out and sitting in some five-star restaurant all alone was not appealing. So I stayed in my room and watched a badly dubbed French version of *Going My Way* on TV.

I called down to the desk and asked for a cab at eight in the morning. My flight wasn't until eleven, but for the first time in my life I was eager to leave Paris. As I lay in bed attempting to sleep I tried to replay the movie of my afternoon at the Hôtel Debussy, but it was gone—like a dream that you can barely remember when you wake up.

For a change, there was no traffic out to De Gaulle. The cab deposited me in front of the TWA terminal at 8:40. I had at least an hour and a half to kill before they called the flight. I checked my bag and wandered around the duty-free shop looking for something to buy my wife before realizing that buying her a Hermès scarf would be sending the wrong signal.

Then I went into the newsstand to get a copy of the *Herald Tribune.* For a few minutes I browsed absently among the magazines, adrift on the low humming noise of people speaking different languages around me.

Within this sound blur, the flat tones of my fellow Americans stuck out. One kid in particular had a loud, insistent voice. "Mom," he whined, "come *on.*"

I looked up across the magazine racks and saw a sandy-haired American kid, eight or nine years old, tugging on his mother's arm. My eyes followed the arm up to the mother.

She was on the tall side, maybe five seven, with long blond hair tied behind her back. Her skin was fair, lightly freckled, and she had off-blue eyes and an interesting mouth. It was an eclectic mixture of features. Iowa mixed with Finland and maybe a touch of Poland.

We locked eyes. As the kid continued to tug on her arm, she gave me a look that was both sad and bemused. I don't know how long we stood there staring at each other across the magazine racks. Maybe two seconds, maybe ten.

A man in Bermuda shorts, sweatshirt, and sneakers walked in. He went up to her and said, with some impatience, "Karen, they're calling our flight. Come on."

Without looking back, she followed him and the boy outside. She was wearing baggy slacks, flats, and a cable-knit sweater that no buyer for Saks would be caught dead in. If you bumped into her backing away from a Monet, you probably would have said "excuse me," turned around, and walked away.

As I watched her head toward the gate with her husband and son, they announced that Flight 378 for Cleveland was in its final boarding stage.

*   *   *

It was a long flight home. We were delayed two hours by weather and then hit headwinds over the Atlantic. I sat next to a very attractive woman in a Chanel suit and Manolo Blahnik heels.[88]

---

[88]$650 and up.

She smiled at me when they brought the drinks. We chatted pleasantly as we sipped cocktails and munched roasted cashews. She was an investment banker from New York, she said. She lived on Central Park West. The ring finger of her left hand was unadorned. She made sure I could see it.

Her name was Rhonda.

CODA

The past is a foreign country; they do things differently there.

—L. P. Hartley

*A*fter *Karen Hôtel Debussy*, there were no more Karens in my life. I remarried—a wonderful woman, for whom reading this book will undoubtedly be a trial—and have been living in unadulterated sainthood, at least as far as the French are concerned, ever since. I have a son by my first marriage, who probably won't be terribly comfortable with this book either. And then there's my mother, who is over ninety, still reads, and has not yet forgotten my proposal of marriage to her during the Vietnam War.

To them I offer only the consolation, if it is one, that I couldn't tell them what is true and what is invented in this book even if I wanted to. Whether consciously or subconsciously, truth and fiction have become blended into a broth that is neither wholly one nor wholly the other. As the years go by and as the past sinks further into the oubliette of time, any hope of disentangling the two becomes more and more problematic.

I think about my son, now in his early twenties, embarking on his life's journey, and I wonder who his Karens will be. I hope they are worthy of him. And vice versa.

And I think about my Karens, scattered to the winds and connected only by my imperfect memory. I wonder what books they would write if they chose to, and what memories they have, of our time together.

Perhaps I am just a footnote in their lives or, worse, completely forgotten.

I would hope, nevertheless, that now and then, after a lovely sunset or the adagio movement from Tchaikovsky's *Romeo and Juliet,* they take a moment to remember. Because, in the end, our lives are the sum of these moments, good or bad. The rest is just bookkeeping.

So, Karens, wherever you are, if you read this, forgive me the liberties I have taken with our stories. I have loved you all, briefly perhaps, imperfectly perhaps, but without design or dissimulation.

It is usually when I'm alone late at night, a little drunk, that I have these thoughts. And for a moment I bring them back to life and feel as if I could actually still touch them. But then I fall asleep. And when I wake up they're gone again to wherever it is that Karens go in the morning.

About the Author

PETER LEFCOURT is the author of five eclectically disreputable novels: *The Woody, Abbreviating Ernie, Di and I, The Dreyfus Affair,* and *The Deal.* He is also an award-winning writer for film and television. He lives in Los Angeles.